Table of contents

DEDICATION

Dedication

*To the ones who turned the page despite the warnings… To the brave souls who chose to enter the hostel, unaware they'd never leave the same… This story isn't just written for you— It's written **with** you.*

Every breath you held, every shadow you imagined in the dark, Fed the ones who live beneath the bed.

You weren't just a reader. You were a part of it.

And if… if the whispers follow you after this… Don't blame the book. It only opened the door.

PROLOGUE

Prologue

The Meeting That Changed Everything

The room was colder than she expected.

Maya clutched her purse to her chest, the tremble in her fingers betraying her calm appearance. The school office was dimly lit, its windows covered in thick velvet drapes. The only light came from a rusted chandelier, swaying slightly as if something had just passed underneath it.

A woman in a grey saree stood by the door. "Please wait. The principal will see you now."

Maya gave a silent nod. Her heart thudded like a trapped bird.

She didn't want to be here.

But what choice did she have?

The door creaked open, revealing a large, old-fashioned office. Books lined the walls, but none had titles. In the center sat a woman with silver-streaked hair tied into a neat bun. Her glasses were perched low on her nose, and her gaze—sharp, knowing—immediately pinned Maya to the floor.

"You must be Maya," the principal said. Her voice was calm, almost gentle. "Please, sit."

Maya lowered herself into the stiff chair, her knuckles white around the strap of her bag. "I… I don't know how to begin," she whispered.

The principal smiled faintly. "Then don't. I already know."

Maya's throat tightened. "She's not a bad girl. Arya. She's just… she's not herself. Ever since that night—"

"You mean the night with the puppies?" the principal interrupted. Her tone was still pleasant, almost motherly.

Maya flinched.

"How did you know—?"

"Some things echo, Maya. Some acts leave stains on the soul. We see them. We hear them. Children like Arya… they call to places like ours."

Maya's lips parted, but no words came.

"You're scared of her, aren't you?"

Silence.

Then a small, broken, "Yes."

The principal rose from her chair and walked slowly toward Maya, her footsteps soundless. She placed a pale hand on Maya's shoulder.

"You did the right thing coming here. Our school is… special. We don't punish. We don't restrain. We reveal."

Maya swallowed. "Will she be safe?"

A pause. A smile.

"She will become who she was always meant to be."

Maya frowned. "I just want her to heal. To forget what she did. To live a normal life. I want her to come back to me."

The principal's eyes flickered. "She won't."

"What?"

"I mean… she won't be the same. No one ever is after this place." Her voice was like velvet wrapped around thorns. "She will be stronger. Closer to her truth. You must understand, Maya—some children aren't born broken. They are born… chosen."

Maya's breath hitched. Her instincts screamed at her to leave. To run. To take Arya far away from this place. But she didn't.

Because deep down… she knew the truth.

Her daughter wasn't normal.

And something inside her was growing darker.

The principal returned to her seat.

"Room 3C is ready," she said with finality. "She'll arrive tomorrow. You may go."

Maya stood on shaking legs, hesitated, and turned one last time.

"What do you see when you look at her?" she asked.

The principal's eyes gleamed like obsidian.

"I see… the beginning."

1:THE FIRST DAY

It's my first time here… in this room. The scent in the air feels oddly familiar. I glance around—three beds. I raise an eyebrow. *"Two more, huh?"* I mutter to myself. It's my first day, and I haven't met my warden yet. I just hope she's cool.

Suddenly, the gate creaks open behind me. I turn to see a girl walk in, dressed in a white mini skirt and a loose t-shirt. Her long hair sways as she moves, and for a moment, she almost looks like a real-life Barbie.

"Hey, are you Arya?" she asks with a soft smile.

I return a faint one of my own and nod. "I'm Arya sharma"

The girl introduced herself as Elina

Elina said she'd show me around, so I followed her through the dim corridors of the hostel. Her voice was light and cheerful, but something about the way she moved—so perfectly poised, so sure of every step— made my skin prickle.

As we walked, I started noticing things. Every girl we passed wore the same outfit: a white skirt and a loose t-shirt, just like Elina's. They all looked eerily alike too—long hair, flawless skin, painted-on smiles. Their eyes lingered on me a little too long. Some whispered. Some giggled. But all of them smiled.

At me.

It felt wrong. Forced. Like I was being welcomed into something I hadn't agreed to.

I tried to ignore it. *Don't overthink it,* I told myself. *It's just a new place. You're nervous. That's all.*

But then we reached the mess hall.

The air smelled of boiled rice and something metallic. My footsteps slowed as I stepped inside and took it all in. The room was huge, echoing with the sound of clinking trays and metal benches scraping the floor. A long line of girls stood waiting for food, their faces blank, almost robotic.

Then the line started moving.

That's when everything changed.

The second food touched their plates, they pounced. Girls dropped to their knees, tearing into the food with their hands, chewing, gulping, snarling like wild animals. It wasn't just hunger—it was desperation, madness. Like they hadn't eaten in days.

I felt my heart slam against my ribs. My feet wanted to move—either run or turn away—but I was frozen.

Elina leaned in, still smiling like everything was normal. "You'll get used to it," she said.

I didn't answer. Because in that moment, I wasn't sure I wanted to.

Elina's smile didn't falter, even as I recoiled from the mess hall chaos. I could still hear the frantic sounds of girls devouring their meals—tearing into their food like they hadn't eaten in days. I stood frozen, heart pounding, barely able to process what I had just witnessed.

"Don't worry, you'll get used to it," Elina repeated, her tone still light, as though we hadn't just seen something that felt like pure madness.

I nodded, though I wasn't sure I could ever *get used* to that. It felt wrong. *Unnatural.*

"Let's head back to the room. You've had a long day," Elina said, guiding me back down the corridor. Her cheerful demeanor hadn't shifted. As if everything was normal. *Was it just me, or was she acting a little too… calm?*

The walk back to the room felt longer than it should've. The lights flickered above us, casting strange shadows along the walls, and every step felt like I was moving deeper into something I couldn't understand.

When we reached the door to our room, Elina pushed it open and gestured for me to enter. "I'll be just a minute," she said, closing the door behind her as she stepped out to grab something from the hallway.

I walked over to the bed and sank down, trying to calm my racing thoughts. I wasn't sure what I was feeling—confusion? Fear? Everything about this place was off, but I didn't have enough answers to make sense of it.

Suddenly, the sound of distant laughter echoed down the hallway. I stood and walked to the window, peering through the blinds. I could see a few girls outside in the courtyard, laughing and talking, all wearing the same outfits. The moonlight made everything seem too perfect, too still. Their voices were sharp, almost too loud, but something about their laughter made my stomach churn.

A sudden knock on the door snapped me out of my thoughts. I opened it to find Elina standing there, holding a tray of food. "You didn't eat much earlier," she said, offering me a soft smile. "Thought you might be hungry." I took the tray hesitantly. The food didn't look bad—boiled rice, a piece of bread, and what looked like a small portion of stew. But something about it, after what I had seen in the mess hall, made my appetite vanish. Still, I forced myself to take a bite.

"Thanks," I said, though the words felt hollow in my mouth.

"Get some rest," Elina added, her smile still wide. "Big day tomorrow."

I nodded, though I wasn't sure what tomorrow would bring. I placed the tray on the small table beside my bed and lay down, staring up at the ceiling. The bed felt too soft, too perfect. It was as if everything here was designed to lull you into a false sense of calm.

But I wasn't calm. Not at all.

As I drifted off to sleep, I couldn't shake the feeling that something terrible was waiting for me tomorrow. And I had no idea how deep this nightmare was about to go.

2:THE CLASSROOM

A sharp knock on the door jolted me awake.

I blinked against the morning light flooding in through the white curtains. My head throbbed slightly—maybe from the weird dreams or maybe just the unfamiliar mattress. I sat up slowly and glanced around the room.

Elina was already up, brushing her hair in front of the mirror. She wore the same outfit again—white skirt, loose t-shirt, spotless like it had just come from a dry cleaner. She looked completely calm, her expression unreadable.

"Morning," she said, catching my eye in the mirror. "You should get ready. We have school today." "School?" I echoed, still half-asleep.

"Yep. You're in Class 12-C. I already checked for you." She tossed me another set of the same white clothes. "Uniforms are mandatory."

Of course they are.

By the time I stepped out of the room, the hallways were already buzzing. Girls moved in lines—tight, silent lines. Every single one of them wore the same outfit, walked at the same pace, even blinked at the same time. It felt less like a school and more like a factory conveyor belt.

Elina disappeared into a crowd, leaving me to find my way.

When I entered **Class 12-C**, it was... quiet. Too quiet.

Every girl in the room looked up when I stepped in. Their heads turned in perfect unison, like puppets. I froze for a second, then walked toward an empty seat near the window. As I sat, I noticed it—scratching. Constant scratching. Some girls kept rubbing their arms, their legs, like something was crawling under their skin.

A few of them looked pale. *No, not pale... cold.* One girl in the corner had goosebumps all over her arms, even though the room wasn't chilly at all. She sat hunched, staring down, lips slightly parted, like she hadn't spoken in years.

What is wrong with them?

Before I could gather my thoughts, another set of doors creaked open.

The boys entered.

They came in through the opposite gate—almost like they weren't supposed to mix with us. They wore white pants and white t-shirts, just like us, only their presence felt... different. They were loud, careless. Some laughed too hard, some kept their heads low, and a few had the kind of faces you'd remember for all the wrong reasons.

A few of them looked dangerous. Angry. Their eyes scanned the room like they were sizing everyone up.

But then—there were a few who looked… normal. Handsome even. One had soft brown eyes and a beard that made him look older than the rest. He smiled at no one, just walked in calmly and took a seat.

That's when I noticed it. **All of them had beards.** No exceptions.

Weird.

The girls didn't look at the boys. No eye contact. No whispers. No reactions. Just that same blank stare, some of them still scratching themselves like it was second nature.

I looked around, trying to make sense of this place.

Whatever this school was, it wasn't normal.

And I had a feeling things were about to get a whole lot worse.

I had barely settled into my seat when I noticed him—slipping into the chair right next to me.

He didn't say a word. Didn't even look my way.

He just sat down with this calm, almost lazy energy, legs stretched out like he owned the place. But what sent a chill down my spine wasn't his silence. It was the soft *clink* of metal.

I looked down.

His ankles were shackled.

Heavy, silver chains peeked out from under his white pants, connected to a black strap fastened around the leg of the desk. I blinked. Was this some kind of punishment? A sick joke? Nobody else even looked surprised.

He leaned back slightly, resting one arm on the edge of his desk, the other busy inspecting his nails like this was all totally normal. His fingers were long, his knuckles bruised. His jaw was sharp, dusted with a thick beard, and there was something in his expression—something unreadable but tense, like a wolf in a cage.

I could feel it—the heat radiating off him. The *presence*. And weirdly… something about him felt *familiar*.

I stole a glance at his face. Still no eye contact.

Do I know him?

But my mind was blank. No memory came. Just this strange pull in my gut, like I was supposed to remember… but couldn't.

Around us, the other students continued their strange rituals. One girl was gently banging her head against the desk in a slow rhythm. Another boy kept muttering numbers under his breath. The pale girl in the corner hadn't moved at all. The scratching noises were constant, almost like background music now.

And then—the door creaked open.

Everyone stopped.

A man entered the room. Tall, lean, dressed in a perfectly ironed grey coat. He carried no books. Just a small leather-bound file.

He walked to the front of the class, eyes scanning us all with the dead calm of a predator. His face was unreadable, but his presence made the air heavy.

"Good morning, students," he said, voice low and sharp. "I am Mr. Yusuf. Your behavioral instructor." *Behavioral instructor?*

I blinked. What kind of subject was that?

The shackled boy beside me finally moved—just barely. He cracked his neck and let out a slow sigh, but still didn't speak.

Mr. Yusuf's eyes landed on him for a split second, something tense passing between them.

This wasn't a school.

This was something else.

And I had no idea what I'd gotten myself into.

"I don't like noise. I don't like hesitation. And I don't like lies," he said, glancing around the room. "This isn't your average classroom, and I'm not your average teacher." A girl coughed.

Yusuf's eyes snapped toward her. "Out."

She stood immediately and walked out in silence. No protest. No second glance. Like she knew the punishment and had accepted it before she made the sound.

I shifted in my seat.

"This week's focus," Yusuf continued, "is communication. Pair activity. You'll each have five minutes to sit face-to-face with a classmate and… talk." *Talk?* That seemed harmless—almost too harmless.

"But remember," he added, eyes gleaming, "truth is mandatory. We'll know if you lie."

The students didn't react. No sighs, no murmurs. Just quiet compliance.

"Start. First pair—Roll number 6 and 7. Veer, Arya."

My breath caught.

Veer?

I turned slowly, and sure enough, the shackled guy—still lounging next to me—finally sat up straighter. His eyes flicked up from his nails, landing on mine for the first time.

And that's when I felt it again.

That strange familiarity.

His gaze wasn't just intense—it was *searching*. Like he was trying to find something in me, something he wasn't even sure existed.

Without a word, he turned his chair toward mine, resting his elbows on his knees. I followed, my movements stiffer, unsure. We sat face-to-face, inches apart, while the rest of the class began their quiet murmured conversations.

Five minutes. Just five.

"You look scared," he said, voice low and deep, a flicker of a smile ghosting his lips.

I held my ground. "I'm not."

He chuckled once—dry, humorless.

"Good. You'll need that."

I didn't know what he meant. I wasn't even sure if he was talking to me or just... talking.

"I'm Arya Sharma," I said cautiously, following the assignment's rule. "You?"

"Veer," he replied, with no last name. Just the name. Like it was a warning in itself.

Something about the way he said it made my skin crawl, but not in fear. In confusion. I knew that name. I had heard it—long ago. In whispers behind my mother's locked door. In arguments I wasn't supposed to hear.

No. It can't be.

But before I could ask anything, Mr. Yusuf clapped once.

"Switch."

Veer stood up immediately and walked back to his place, chains softly clinking with every step. No glance back. No more words.

And yet—I couldn't stop looking at him.

He didn't know who I was. And I didn't know who he *really* was.

Not someone known

3:RULES

After class, Elina tugged at my sleeve. "Come on," she whispered. "Warden Riana's expecting you."

We walked through dimly lit corridors, every step echoing. It felt like the whole building held its breath. As we reached a narrow hall, the scent changed—antiseptic and something metallic underneath.

Then she appeared.

Warden Riana.

She stood at the far end of the corridor like she'd materialized out of the walls. Her frame was tall and thin, almost unnaturally so. Her grey dress looked starched to the point of stiffness, her lips painted a bloodless shade of mauve. Her eyes were... glassy. Like she was always staring just past you.

"Elina," she said in a clipped tone. "Wait outside."

"Yes, ma'am," Elina whispered and stepped back.

I followed the warden into her office. The walls were bone white. No pictures. No noise. Just a clock ticking way too slowly.

She gestured to the chair across from her and sat with her hands folded neatly on the desk.

"You are Arya Sharma," she stated, not asked.

I nodded.

"We do not tolerate disobedience here. You will follow our structure. Without question. Without delay."

Then she began listing the rules—each one more bizarre than the last:

No mirrors allowed. Every reflective surface is removed. "They invite confusion," she said flatly.

Clothes must be folded in sets of threes. No more. No less.

You must sleep facing the wall. Always.

You are not to make physical contact with other students unless given permission.

During 'Night Hours,' no one leaves their bed. Not for the bathroom. Not for anything.

One hour before lights-out, no talking. You must sit on your bed. And reflect.

If the bell rings once after midnight—ignore it.

"Do you understand?" she asked, tilting her head just a little too far.

"I… I guess," I said, unsure.

"Guessing is not permitted," she said, her voice colder now. "We require certainty here."

Then she stood. "Your room is on the third floor. Room 306. Elina is your roommate. Do not ask about the third bed."

I blinked. "What? But—"

"Do. Not. Ask."

The finality in her voice silenced me.

As I stepped out, Elina was already waiting.

She didn't speak until we reached our room. The number 306 was scratched slightly, like someone had clawed at the door. Inside, it was eerily clean. Three beds. Two bags.

Elina helped me settle in, folding my clothes robotically.

I couldn't stop staring at the third bed.

It was perfectly made. White sheet tucked tight. Pillow untouched. Like a ghost slept there. Or someone still *might*.

"Elina," I said carefully, "who uses that bed?"

She stiffened.

"No one."

"Is it… for someone new?"

She paused for too long.

"It's just… not used. But don't mess it up. Seriously. Don't touch it. And whatever happens, never sleep in it."

"Why?"

She looked me dead in the eye. "Because she doesn't like that."

I froze. "Who?"

Elina turned away. "Just… don't ask questions, Arya. Not about her. Not about the bed. And not when the lights go out."

I didn't press further.

But that night, I couldn't sleep.

Because every time I turned toward that third bed i swore i saw the blanket shift just a little

The room was silent. Too silent. Like even the walls were holding their breath.

I lay stiffly on my bed, **facing the wall**, just as the rule demanded. Elina's soft breathing came from the other side of the room. Rhythmic. Controlled. I envied her ability to sleep in this nightmare.

But I couldn't.

My eyes were open, locked on the blank wall in front of me. And that third bed... it hadn't made a sound all night. Not a rustle. Not a creak.

Until now.

Creak.

The noise was barely there, like the slow bending of wood under pressure. I told myself it was nothing.

Then I felt it.

The bed dipped.

Not mine. **The third one.**

A low groan of the mattress followed, like someone heavy had just sat on it. My heart stopped. My entire body went cold. But I didn't move. I couldn't.

The rule.

Do not turn. Do not look away from the wall.

And then... **I felt the weight.** On **my** bed.

Like something—or someone—had crawled in behind me.

The mattress shifted with each slow, crawling movement. My breath hitched. I didn't dare inhale too loudly.

Then... **cold fingers brushed the back of my neck.**

I froze.

The touch was soft. Too soft. Like fingertips wrapped in silk, gliding slowly, as if *exploring* me.

And then I felt the other hand—**pressing flat against my back.**

Firm. Unmoving.

Like it was pinning me down.

I wanted to scream. I wanted to **turn**. But I couldn't. My mind screamed the rule over and over:

"You must sleep facing the wall. Always."

The hand started to crawl upward—shoulder… neck… hair.

Then it stopped.

And a breath, hot and sharp, brushed against my ear.

A whisper. **"You're in my bed."**

I shut my eyes so tight they burned. My fists clenched under the blanket, and I forced my breathing to stay quiet, even as my body trembled beneath the touch.

After what felt like an hour, the weight lifted.

The mattress rose back into place. The air returned to normal. The room was silent again.

But I didn't sleep.

Not a single second.

Because I knew—**someone** had been in that bed. And maybe still was.

Watching me. Waiting for me to break the rule.

Morning came, but it didn't feel like it.

The light that filtered through the curtains was dim and grey, like even the sun was afraid to shine too brightly here. I hadn't slept. Not even a blink. I just lay there, waiting for Elina to move, waiting for any sign that what happened wasn't real.

She finally stirred, sitting up with a yawn like it was just another normal day in hell.

"You didn't sleep," she said softly, looking at my pale face.

I nodded slowly, unsure how to even speak.

Her gaze drifted toward the third bed. Her voice dropped to a whisper.

"You felt her… didn't you?"

I stared at her.

She didn't look surprised. She didn't even look scared.

"You said no one uses that bed," I whispered.

"No one **alive** does," she said, eyes locked on mine.

My stomach twisted.

Elina stood, grabbed her towel and uniform, and headed toward the bathroom like it was any regular day.

Before leaving, she paused in the doorway and looked back. "You're lucky," she said. "She didn't stay."

And just like that, she was gone.

I sat there frozen, still facing the wall, wondering how long I could survive in a place where even the **beds had ghosts**.

4:THE GIRL WHO SMILED MUCH

I always thought I was a happy child. I smiled a lot. Maybe too much. But it never felt like something to worry about. I liked smiling. It made everything seem okay, even when it wasn't.

I was twelve when things started to change. The days before everything got blurry… before everything got wrong.

My mother and I lived in a house on the edge of town, a house that always smelled faintly of vanilla and old books. I was alone a lot. She worked late, came home tired. We didn't speak much. I had my room, filled with books, dolls, and a mirror I would stare into for hours. It was like I could see something in the reflection that wasn't really there, something watching me.

I had friends at school. Two girls—Annie and Priya. We'd laugh and play at lunch, and they'd tell me I was always so happy. I didn't understand why that made them nervous sometimes. I liked their smiles too, so I kept mine wide.

But teachers… they didn't like me smiling all the time.

Once, I sat still in my seat for hours. My eyes didn't blink. I didn't move. Just staring. Mrs. Patel noticed, but I didn't say anything. I don't remember the feeling, just the quiet. The stillness.

Another time, I wrote in my notebook for hours. Pages and pages, just one sentence over and over again: **"They don't bleed like we do."**

I didn't know what it meant. I didn't even remember writing it until they showed me the pages.

It was early March when the puppies came to school. Everyone was excited. We were allowed to bring in pets—puppies, kittens, anything. My heart was beating faster that day, but I didn't know why. It was a good kind of fast.

I liked animals. I liked how soft their fur felt, how they looked up at you with wide eyes, trusting.

But that afternoon, I was inside when the others went out to play. I don't know why I didn't go with them. I don't remember.

The first time I noticed something wrong was the smell. I hadn't realized it until I was standing in the middle of the room, surrounded by the puppies, their tiny bodies lifeless on the floor. My hands were covered in blood, but I didn't understand. I wasn't scared. I just felt curious, like I wanted to know why they stopped moving.

It wasn't until I saw the teacher's face—white with shock—that I realized something was wrong. But I didn't know what.

"I was feeding them," I said. "But they stopped moving."

That's what I told her. She didn't say anything, but she was shaking, so I knew I had done something bad. But I didn't mean to. I didn't.

The next few days were a blur. They kept asking me questions I couldn't answer. But I didn't feel like I needed to. I smiled through it all, but the smiles weren't the same anymore. Something inside me felt heavy. Something dark and **silent**.

Then came the missing kids.

Priya and Annie were gone that day, gone like they had never existed. At first, I didn't care. I thought they'd just gone home early. But when the teachers said they were missing, I started to worry. Where had they gone? Why didn't anyone know?

It wasn't until the janitor found them—locked in a supply closet—that I realized something wasn't right. They were cold, their faces bruised, their lips purple. They were still, like they were asleep, but their bodies said they weren't.

I didn't understand. Why hadn't they just left? Why were they *here*?

When they asked me where I'd been, I said I was in the library. They didn't believe me. No one did.

I don't remember anything after that. It's like there's a fog. A thick haze that blurs everything after I left the classroom that day. The last thing I remember is standing in the hallway, feeling something on my face—cold, wet—but when I wiped it, it was blood.

My mother's reaction was the same as always—silent, distant. She never told me what was going on in her head. But I could see the fear in her eyes. The way she started to distance herself from me.

By the time I turned seventeen, I had seen more doctors and psychologists than I could count. They all said the same thing: "She's fine." But then they'd say, "Maybe not normal. Maybe a little too quiet. Maybe too… unpredictable."

They never really knew what to do with me. They gave me pills, different therapies, all sorts of treatments. But nothing worked. I wasn't broken in their eyes. I wasn't crazy. At least, not enough to fix.

That's when she sent me here. To the place where everything started to get… even more strange.

The car ride to the school was silent. My mother's hands were stiff on the wheel. I wanted to ask where we were going, but I didn't. I had never asked her much. I didn't think she'd answer.

When we finally arrived at the gates, she stopped the car but didn't look at me. She opened the door for me and said the same words she'd whispered before. "I hope they can fix you."

I didn't understand. I smiled, like I always did.

She drove away without a second glance. I stood there, staring after her until the dust from the gravel road settled. And then I turned back to face the gates of the school. My new life.

But someone had been watching me. Someone who knew me. Someone who was always there.

He had been part of the school for years, a fixture, always there but never quite visible. Always just out of reach.

I didn't know it then, but **he** was part of my past. The one I could never remember. The one who had disappeared from my life.

5:THE THIRD BED

I woke up gasping.

It was like someone had pulled the breath right out of my chest. For a moment, I couldn't remember where I was. The dim morning light filtered in through the iron-barred window, casting long shadows across the floor. My heart pounded, and I reached behind me instinctively—nothing.

But last night… Last night, **someone was there**. I felt it. Cold, crawling hands tracing my spine. A heavy presence lying against my back. A breath that didn't belong to me. I wasn't dreaming—I *know* I wasn't dreaming.

But now the bed was empty. Still. Quiet.

And the third bed across from me… untouched. As if no one had ever laid on it. As if it waited.

I swallowed the lump in my throat and sat up. Elina's bed was empty. She was already gone, probably getting ready in the washroom or in the common area. I glanced at the third bed again, trying to shake the unease twisting inside my stomach.

I knew the rule: *face the wall while sleeping.* But no one said what would happen if you did.

I clenched my fists and climbed down from my bed, trying to steady my breathing. The cold tiles beneath my feet only added to the chill I couldn't shake.

When I stepped into the common room, Elina was seated on the long wooden bench, braiding her hair in front of the mirror. Her expression was calm, almost blank—but too calm.

"Good morning," she said softly without turning to look at me.

"Morning," I muttered. I didn't know how to bring it up. How do you ask someone if a ghost laid behind you in the middle of the night?

So I said the only thing that made sense. "Elina… I couldn't sleep."

She finally turned to me. Her dark eyes locked on mine in the mirror. "Nightmares?" she asked, though something in her tone suggested she already knew the answer.

I shook my head. "No… Not exactly. I—" I hesitated. "Elina… last night, it felt like… someone was lying behind me."

She froze mid-braid. Her fingers tightened around the strands of her hair.

"I couldn't move. I remembered the rule. But I felt… hands. Cold. Breathing. I wasn't alone."

For a second, Elina didn't say anything. She turned back toward the mirror, resuming her braiding as if I hadn't just said something terrifying.

"You must've been dreaming," she said finally, her voice too light, too forced.

"I wasn't," I whispered.

Silence stretched between us. Then she said, without looking at me, "You shouldn't think too much about the third bed."

My heart skipped. "So… you *know* it's not normal?"

She gave a small nod. "It's just how things are here. Some things don't need explanations, Arya. They just need obedience."

Obedience.

That word echoed in my mind, ugly and sharp. Like everything about this place.

"Elina, who's supposed to sleep there?" I asked, lowering my voice.

She looked up at me this time, really looked. "No one."

I didn't believe her.

She stood and walked toward the door. "Get dressed. You don't want to miss meeting Mr. Yusuf. Trust me—he hates latecomers."

And then she left, just like that.

I sat back down on the edge of my bed. My eyes drifted to the third one again. Not a crease. Not a pillow out of place. Perfectly made. Perfectly still.

Who was in my bed last night? What would've happened if I turned around? And why did Elina sound like she was scared to say more?

There were too many questions.

And this place? This place was more than just strict rules and creepy vibes. It was *wrong*. Something in its walls watched you, listened, waited. I could feel it like pressure under my skin.

As I pulled on my uniform and tied my hair back, I knew one thing for sure.

I needed to find out what was really going on. Before whatever was in that bed… decided to get closer.

I kept my head down as I walked through the corridor, still shaken from last night. The sunlight that spilled through the stained glass windows didn't warm the air. It felt like the light here couldn't reach the cold.

I followed the others—girls in white skirts and shirts, walking silently like dolls in a parade. Not one of them looked at me. Not one smiled. It was like I didn't exist.

But their eyes had been all over me yesterday.

We reached the main building. My class was 12th-C. The door was half open, creaking ever so slightly. I hesitated before stepping in.

And that's when I saw him.

He sat alone, near the back of the room.

Tall. Broad shoulders. Hair a mess of dark curls that almost reached his eyes. His wrists were free, but his **ankles were bound in thick iron shackles**, heavy chains trailing against the floor. He didn't look up. His head was tilted down, eyes locked on his fingernails—long, sharp, as if he was trying to claw something out of his skin.

Something about him made my stomach twist. Not just his presence, but… something *familiar*. Like I had seen him in a dream once. Or a nightmare.

The others were already seated. Girls to one side. Boys to the other. Everyone looked strange—scratching their arms constantly, twitching, whispering things to themselves. Some had eyes like fogged glass. Others didn't blink at all.

I took a seat at the front, trying not to stare, but I could feel his presence behind me like heat on my neck.

"His name's Veer," a girl beside me whispered. Her voice was flat, as if she was reading a line someone told her to memorize. "He's been here the longest. Don't talk to him."

"Why?" I asked before I could stop myself.

She didn't answer. Just looked away and started drawing circles on her desk with her nail.

I glanced over my shoulder again. Veer hadn't moved. But his eyes— dark, hollow, alive—were now **on me**.

I looked away instantly.

Why did it feel like he *knew* me?

Before I could make sense of anything, the classroom door slammed shut. Mr. Yusuf had arrived.

He walked with a stiff, robotic rhythm. Dressed all in black, bald head gleaming under the dim light. His eyes scanned the class, unblinking.

"Silence," he said, and the entire class went dead still.

"We'll begin with communication drills today. No talking unless spoken to. You will face your assigned partners and answer only the questions I permit."

I shifted in my seat. Assigned partners?

Please not him, I prayed.

But of course, when he called my name—"Arya Sharma"—the second name that followed was, "Veer."

My heart stopped.

Everyone turned to look. Even the ones who hadn't blinked all day. Veer stood up slowly, the **sound of chains dragging** echoing across the floor like metal teeth scraping bone.

He took the seat across from me.

Still didn't speak.

But his eyes were *reading me.*

I couldn't move. Couldn't breathe. There was something in his gaze that felt *off.* Not cruel. Not angry.

Just… broken. Familiar.

And so cold.

"Begin," Mr. Yusuf said.

Veer leaned forward, just slightly. His voice, when it came, was deep—like gravel soaked in smoke. "Do you remember me?"

I blinked. My lips parted. "W-What?"

He said nothing more.

Not until Mr. Yusuf passed behind us. Then Veer's mouth moved again.

But his voice didn't match his lips.

In that moment, I realized something terrifying:

He wasn't speaking *with* his mouth.

He was speaking inside my **head**.

"Do you remember me?" the voice echoed again.

I pushed back in my chair, heart pounding in my throat.

What the hell was this place?

And *who* was Veer?

6:THE HOLLOW GAME

Mr. Yusuf's voice echoed across the class. "Arya. Veer. You'll complete the communication exercise together. Room Eleven."

Heads turned. Whispers stirred. My chest tightened.

Veer didn't move at first, then stood slowly. His shackles dragged faintly against the ground—metal against stone. Still silent. Still unreadable.

I followed.

The door at the end of the corridor groaned open. Darkness spilled out like smoke.

"Ten minutes," Mr. Yusuf said. "No sound unless spoken to. Don't touch anything."

I stepped in after Veer. The door slammed behind me.

Total darkness.

I couldn't even see my hand in front of me. The air felt thick—almost like it pulsed. I heard Veer breathe somewhere nearby.

Then, finally, his voice broke the silence.

"You're not scared of the dark?" he asked quietly.

I hesitated. "I'm… used to it."

He chuckled—low, bitter.

"I doubt that."

We stood there, wrapped in the nothingness. His voice again:

"Do you ever feel like there's something inside you you can't explain?"

My throat tightened. "What do you mean?"

"Like… a voice. A shadow. Something that doesn't feel like you."

I swallowed. "That's… a strange question."

"I ask strange questions," he said, and I could hear the smile in his tone. "You're not like the others."

"You don't even know me."

"I've known you longer than you think."

My heart skipped.

"What does that mean?"

Silence.

And then, slowly, his footsteps circled around me. I could feel him behind me—close, but not touching.

"Do you believe people are born evil?" he asked.

I didn't answer.

"Or do they just wake up one day… and stop being human?"

I wanted to leave. I wanted to scream. But I couldn't move. The rules. The silence. The weight of his words.

"You're asking the wrong questions," I said shakily.

He stepped closer. "Maybe you're just scared to hear the answers."

Then—light. Harsh and sudden.

Mr. Yusuf stood at the door, face blank.

"Return to class."

Veer walked out without another word.

I followed, my mind spinning. There were no secrets in that room… but there were hints. Shadows.

And something in the way he spoke made my blood boil

The silence stretched between us like a wire pulled too tight. Then Veer spoke again, softer this time.

"You've felt it before, haven't you?"

I turned toward his voice instinctively, but all I saw was blackness. "Felt what?"

"That pull. Like your own body doesn't belong to you sometimes."

My chest tightened. "You don't know anything about me."

He chuckled under his breath. "I know more than you think. You talk in your sleep, you know."

That stopped me.

"No, I don't."

"I've heard you. The way you whisper names. The way you beg for it to stop."

My skin crawled. "You're lying."

"Am I?" he whispered. "Or maybe I just see things the others ignore."

I stepped back. My heel hit the wall.

"You don't know me," I repeated.

"No," he said, his tone almost gentle now. "But I remember the first time you came here. You were just a kid. I was already here."

I swallowed hard. "How could you know that?"

No answer.

"Who *are* you?"

Still no answer.

Then—his voice, close again. Too close.

"I've seen your eyes in the mirror before. You don't remember, but your soul does."

I stiffened. "You're crazy."

"Maybe," he said. "But you will be too. Soon."

"What do you mean?"

His breath tickled the side of my face. I didn't even hear him move.

"Because this place doesn't fix broken things. It *feeds* them."

My hands clenched.

"I'm not broken," I snapped.

Silence.

Then his voice again, colder than before.

"You should be scared of the wall, Arya. Not because you can't face it… but because one day, it might finally face back"

The blinding hallway light felt like punishment as I stepped out. I didn't say a word to Veer. He didn't say one to me. His shackles clinked softly with every step he took back toward the classroom.

I followed behind him, my head buzzing with what he said. *This place doesn't fix broken things. It feeds them.*

The moment I entered, the room fell quiet. The air was colder, heavier —as if the room *knew* something had happened.

The girls in my class stared at me, grinning. Wide. Too wide. Their faces frozen in that plastic way that didn't match their eyes. A few of them whispered to each other, but the sound was...off. Garbled. Like broken records on loop.

One of them, a girl named Reva, leaned closer to her seatmate and whispered, "She was in the room with *him*."

My chair scraped the floor as I pulled it out. I could feel eyes burning into my back.

I sat down, and as if on cue, Veer sat beside me again. His presence was like cold steel pressed against skin. He didn't look at me. Didn't move.

I tried to focus on the board, but something shifted.

Reva, two seats away, started scratching her arm. Not lightly. Violently.

Skin flaked off. Blood showed.

Another girl across the row began to hum—some eerie tune that echoed like a lullaby from a nightmare.

And the boys…

One of them—Ajay, I think—was laughing. Alone. Loud. His fingers twitching like they were typing invisible keys.

The room felt wrong.

This isn't a school. This is a cage.

Mr. Yusuf entered, and everything went still again. Too still. Even the air paused.

"Today," he said, staring directly at me, "you all met your match. Or perhaps... your reflection."

His eyes lingered on me longer than they should have.

"Let's begin," he said with a crooked smile. "Let's see what your minds reveal... when they forget to lie."

I heard Veer chuckle under his breath.

And suddenly, I knew—I wasn't imagining anything.

Something here wanted me broken.

And someone in here already knew how to do it.

The rest of the class dragged on like a nightmare disguised in normalcy. Whispers danced in the air. Fingers twitched. Eyes followed me, even when I wasn't moving.

By the time the bell rang, I felt like I'd survived something I didn't understand.

I stood to leave, but Mr. Yusuf raised a hand.

"Miss Arya," he said, too softly. "Stay a moment."

Veer didn't wait. He walked out, shackles clinking down the hallway.

I approached Mr. Yusuf's desk, heart hammering.

"You're adjusting well," he said. "But let's see how you... *perform* under pressure."

"What do you mean?" I asked.

He smiled. His teeth looked too sharp in the light.

"Tomorrow," he said, "your class will begin *The Hollow Game*."

The air in the room seemed to vanish.

My throat tightened. "What is that?"

But he didn't answer.

Behind me, I heard Reva whisper again. "Not all who play come back the same."

Mr. Yusuf leaned forward. "Sleep well, Arya."

His eyes gleamed.

"You'll need it."

7:I FELT HER

The cold in the hallway seemed to linger, as though the walls themselves were holding their breath. I pulled my jacket tighter around me, feeling a shiver run through my spine as I walked back to the room.

Elina walked beside me, but there was something off about her tonight. Her steps were quieter, her smile more distant, as if she were in her own world. The laughter and whispers from earlier were gone, replaced by an unsettling silence that weighed heavily on the air.

Rule #5: Never walk the halls alone after dark.

I wasn't alone, but it felt like I was.

When we reached Room 17, Elina barely glanced at me before slipping into her bed, pulling the covers over her. Her face, usually full of life and energy, now seemed distant and cold. I couldn't remember the last time I'd heard her laugh. The tension in the room pressed down on me, so thick I could almost taste it.

I stood by the door, my gaze drawn to the third bed again—the one that no one spoke of. The one that was always neatly made, yet never used. The one that made me feel uneasy, as though it were waiting for something… or someone.

I didn't want to look at it, but I couldn't help myself. Something about that bed gnawed at me, a deep, crawling sensation that I couldn't shake. It was almost as if the room itself knew I was thinking about it. The air seemed to grow heavier.

I climbed into bed, my back pressed firmly against the mattress. I turned away from the room, facing the wall like I was supposed to.

Rule #3: Always face the wall while sleeping.

I obeyed. But it didn't feel like enough.

The room seemed to grow colder, and the silence thickened, wrapping around me like a heavy, suffocating blanket. I felt eyes on me. I could almost hear the whispers, but they were muffled, just out of reach.

I tried to push the thoughts away, forcing my mind to shut down, to drift into sleep. But then—

I felt it.

A weight. A shift.

The mattress behind me dipped, as if someone had just sat down. My heart slammed against my chest.

I couldn't turn. I couldn't move.

The rule... The thought was a whisper in my head, a reminder of the ironclad rule I couldn't break.

I tried to ignore it. Tried to breathe through the fear that tightened my throat. But the weight behind me grew, pressing down on the bed, like something—or someone—was lying next to me.

The air turned cold. **Ice cold.**

My skin prickled. My heart raced.

I couldn't do anything. I couldn't move. I couldn't even scream.

And then—slowly, **deliberately**—I felt it.

Cold fingers. **Cold fingers** sliding up my back, as if they had been waiting for the perfect moment to touch me. They were long, thin, too thin. They didn't feel human.

They crept up my spine, one vertebra at a time, sending shivers of ice through my body. The fingers curled over my shoulders, cold and dead, like they were tracing the shape of my body, memorizing it. I wanted to scream, to turn, to push them away, but the rule held me there. Frozen. Helpless.

The whisper came again, this time so close I could feel the breath against my ear.

"Good girls follow the rules..."

It was low. Twisted. A voice that didn't belong to anyone I knew. The sound made my stomach churn, my limbs numb with terror.

It didn't stop there.

The fingers—still crawling—pressed harder, dragging across my skin, up to my neck. I could feel the weight of something behind me, watching me. The bed sank under an unseen weight, and I knew—**knew**—that something was right there, just inches from my face.

I didn't dare to move.

I didn't dare to breathe.

And then, the whisper came again, this time a little too loud.

"Facing the wall won't always save you..."

A laugh.

A laugh.

It wasn't human. It wasn't even close. It was hollow. Empty. Cold.

It echoed in my mind, bouncing off the walls of the room, rattling in my skull.

The cold fingers disappeared as quickly as they had come. The bed rose back to its normal level. The air warmed by a fraction.

It was over. For now.

I didn't dare open my eyes. I didn't dare move.

I stayed perfectly still, heart pounding in my chest, as the silence wrapped around me once more.

But I knew one thing—**I would never look at that third bed the same way again.**

The next morning

I tried to act normal, but the fear still lingered, crawling under my skin. Elina was still asleep when I got up, her breathing soft and steady. I didn't want to disturb her, but I couldn't shake the feeling that something was wrong. The weight of the bed, the cold fingers, the voice—it all felt like a nightmare I couldn't escape.

When I glanced at the third bed again, I could have sworn it looked... **used**.

But no one ever sat there. No one ever slept there.

I wanted to ask Elina about it, but the words caught in my throat. I could feel the silence between us growing. She seemed so distant. She wasn't the same girl I had met when I first arrived.

I climbed out of bed, avoiding looking at the third bed, but I could feel its presence, watching me. **Waiting**.

I was almost out the door when Elina finally stirred.

"Sleep well?" she asked, her voice calm, almost too calm. She gave me a half-smile, but it didn't reach her eyes.

I nodded, though my throat was dry. "Yeah. You?"

She stretched and smiled a little wider. "I sleep fine. Don't worry about the third bed."

My heart skipped a beat.

"I don't," I muttered. But deep down, I was terrified. I couldn't shake the feeling that it wasn't done with me yet.

It was just beginning.

Mr. Yusuf announced something that chilled my blood. "Tomorrow," he said, his voice sharp, his eyes gleaming with something unreadable, "we begin the first round of the Hollow Game."

A hush fell over the class.

I wasn't the only one who had felt the sudden shift in the air.

The Hollow Game? My stomach clenched.

And then, I saw him—Veer. His eyes were fixed on me with an intensity that made my skin crawl. There was something dark in those eyes. Something dangerous.

Whatever the Hollow Game was, I wasn't ready for it.

8:FEAR

They said it was just a game. A classroom activity. Something to "test our courage." But the moment Mr. Yusuf's voice cut through the dead air —*"Welcome to The Hollow Game"*—I knew something was wrong. Not the kind of wrong you feel when you forget your homework. This was the kind of wrong that made your blood freeze. That whispered to you that you weren't safe anymore. That maybe… you never were.

The bell rang. The sharp clang echoed like a scream.

We stood up.

Everyone moved at once. No one asked questions. No one made a sound. Even Elina, who usually whispered jokes or tugged my sleeve, looked...empty. She didn't even glance my way.

I walked behind them, stiff and uncertain, my shoes tapping rhythmically across the cold tile. The corridor we took today was not the one I recognized. This one was darker, narrower, and filled with strange paintings—portraits of children with wide, hollow eyes and faces blurred by time or something more sinister. The walls were wet, as if the building was sweating.

Then we reached the door.

Room 000.

It looked like the entrance to a prison cell. Rust lined the edges of the iron door. A foul smell leaked from inside—something sharp and chemical, mixed with the decay of forgotten things. Mr. Yusuf smiled like this was all very normal. "One by one," he said. "Face your hollows."

The door creaked open. No one touched it.

And they pushed me in first.

Darkness. Thick, suffocating darkness swallowed me whole.

It was not the absence of light. It was *presence*—something alive, breathing, *watching*. My arms extended, trying to find something, *anything*. I couldn't even see my own fingers.

Then the cold came.

Deep, unforgiving cold. The kind that gnaws at your bones. My teeth clattered. I could see my breath like fog in front of my face.

And then, a laugh.

A child's laugh. Soft at first. Then closer.

I froze.

No... no, please not this.

It echoed all around me, bouncing off invisible walls.

"Arya…"

A whisper. Feminine. Familiar. My mother's voice.

I shut my eyes. But I was no longer in the room.

The dark began to twist and shape itself around me. Walls grew from shadows. Light leaked in through a window. A ceiling fan creaked overhead.

I knew this place.

My childhood home.

My two-year-old self sat hidden under the table, trembling. My bare legs folded beneath me. The cold ceramic floor against my skin. I could feel it all as if I was truly there again.

Why am I seeing this?

Then—*crash*. My mother's scream. Sharp, raw, terrified.

I turned.

Veer stood in the middle of the living room. His face wasn't like I remembered from photographs. It was wild. Unrecognizable. His eyes bulged, filled with madness. A knife glittered in his hand.

He pushed her. She fell back, her head hitting the wall. Blood trickled down from her temple. She sobbed, still shielding me with her arms even from a distance.

And then… his voice.

"I love you, Arya. I will take you away. You're mine."

He wasn't talking to my mother.

He was talking to *me*.

The sirens came. Red and blue lights lit up the room. But I never forgot his words. Even as officers tackled him to the ground. Even as they dragged him away. He kept shouting: **"You're mine. I'll come for you. Someday."**

I didn't even realize I was screaming.

I collapsed on the floor of Room 000, crying into my arms. The image wouldn't leave me. That man… Veer… my classmate now. That dangerous, shackled boy who never looked me in the eye.

He was my father.

The memory had been buried. Until now.

But why didn't I remember this before?

Because I was too young? Or because something—someone—*hid* it from me?

Then I heard a whisper again. This time from within the darkness. A man's voice, deep and quiet, as if pressing against my brain: **"You're awakening now. Just like I promised."**

The door burst open.

Light burned my eyes.

Mr. Yusuf stood on the other side, smiling as always, his clipboard in hand. "Next," he said calmly, as if nothing had happened.

I could barely walk as I stepped out. My legs trembled with every step. I felt… hollow. As if something inside me had been scooped out and shown to me under a microscope.

The others didn't speak. No one even glanced at me.

Back in the corridor, I stumbled through the haze of my thoughts.

He's here.

Veer is here.

And he doesn't even know I'm his daughter.

Or… does he?

I thought of his eyes. How sometimes I caught him staring—not at me, but *through* me. As if he was remembering something, too.

Was it really a game?

Or a ritual?

A way to unlock what was buried deep within us?

And if this was just the *beginning* of The Hollow Game… what else would they drag from the darkness?

Back in the corridor, the silence screamed louder than any siren ever could. One by one, the others were sent in. I tried not to count, but I couldn't stop.

Forty rooms. Forty students. Each one alone. Each one to face their **deepest, most unspeakable fear.**

I sat on the cracked bench along the hallway. My eyes stung, not just from the vision I'd just seen, but from the suffocating stillness that followed. Some kids came out gasping for breath. Others—shaking, hollow, bleeding from their nose, ears… One girl collapsed entirely, mumbling words that didn't belong to any language we knew.

And then… twenty never came back.

The doors to their Hollow Rooms never opened again.

The numbers kept decreasing. One. Then two. Then five. Then ten. Mr. Yusuf never flinched. He simply crossed out names on his list as if erasing chalk from a board.

No one asked questions.

Because we all knew.

Something took them.

Or worse—*something stayed behind.*

We were told the rules at the beginning: once you enter your hollow, you leave it empty.

But now I understood what that meant.

The twenty who didn't return had not died in the traditional sense. Their **souls** were gone—trapped behind those steel doors, screaming in silence. And the *things* that had once whispered within them… those demons… those *ancient shadows* that lived inside their bloodlines—they now had no vessel to corrupt.

So the rooms became prisons. **Soul-cages.**

Rooms that still echoed with breathless laughter and whispers that made even the floorboards shiver. Hollow Rooms, they called them now. Locked forever.

And the remaining twenty of us?

We were the "lucky" ones.

But I didn't feel lucky. I felt *haunted.*

Because I knew what lived in me wasn't gone.

It was only… waking up.

9:TRUTH

The silence that followed *The Hollow Game* was louder than the screams of the students I couldn't see. My heart thudded painfully in my chest as I stumbled out of the dark room. My breath was shallow, my body heavy. The shadows had swallowed me whole, but they left something behind. The fear.

It wasn't just the game that haunted me—it was the memory that it had ripped from the back of my mind. The image of my father, *Veer*, looming over my mother with a knife in his hand. I was only two years old, but the memory felt like it had been etched into the deepest parts of my soul.

I could still hear his voice, cold and unwavering.

"I love you, Arya. I will surely take you away."

The words had never left me. They had been buried deep in the darkest part of my mind, locked away behind a door that I hadn't wanted to open. But *The Hollow Game...* it forced me to remember. The fear, the tension, the terror—it was all there again.

I couldn't breathe. I couldn't think.

I walked through the corridor of the school, the walls closing in around me. The whispers of the other students felt too close, too suffocating. Their eyes were on me, *always* on me.

Why?

I passed Room 12, and I heard it again—the giggle. It wasn't a playful one. It was wrong, twisted. The walls seemed to *breathe*, the air thicker than it had been before. There was something lurking in the corners, something waiting.

I kept walking. I needed to escape it. I needed to escape *this place*.

When I got back to my room, I was alone. Elina was nowhere to be seen. I sat on the edge of my bed, staring at the third bed in the room. It was always empty. But today… there was a change.

The blankets were *wrinkled*.

No one had sat on it. No one had touched it, but the bed looked like it had been disturbed.

I felt a chill run through me.

I knew I shouldn't have, but I reached out and touched the blanket. It was cold—colder than the air around me. I withdrew my hand quickly, my pulse racing.

What was happening here? What was this place?

I couldn't stay here. Not after what I had seen, not after the truth that was clawing its way out. The images of my past, the things I had done, the things I didn't *remember*—it was too much. But there was something else— something darker. Something I needed to understand.

I wasn't sure when I decided to follow him.

But I did.

Veer. He had been walking alone in the courtyard, like he knew where he was going. I had seen him before—his shackled legs, his eyes always distant—but today, there was something different about him. I couldn't explain it.

I followed him, my footsteps echoing in the eerie silence.

The courtyard was empty. No other students, no one to stop me. Just the wind, cold and biting. He walked toward the old prayer hall—the one that was locked up, the one that no one was allowed to enter.

I had never been this close to it before.

But Veer… he slipped inside without a second thought.

I stood in front of the door, my heart racing. I couldn't just let him go in alone. I couldn't ignore the nagging feeling that something inside that hall would answer the questions I had been asking.

I pushed the door open. The air was colder inside. Stale, ancient. The darkness wrapped itself around me like a cloak.

Veer was standing in front of an old altar, looking at something—or someone—that I couldn't see.

I stepped forward, my voice trembling. "Veer... what is this place?"

He didn't turn, but his voice was calm, too calm.

"You followed me," he said, his words barely a whisper. "You're breaking rules, Arya."

"I don't care about your rules anymore," I spat, stepping closer. "I need answers."

His silence was the answer.

Then, he turned to face me. His eyes were cold, his face unreadable. "You remember nothing, do you?"

"I remember *enough*," I replied, my voice shaking. "You… you were there. When I was two."

His smile was devoid of warmth. "I remember."

My heart slammed against my chest. "Who are you?"

He didn't answer immediately. He just stared at me, as if weighing something inside his mind. Finally, his lips parted, and his words dripped with coldness.

"Not a father," he said softly. "Not anymore."

I couldn't breathe. "I saw what you made me do. Those puppies… my best friends..."

He took a step closer. The chains around his ankles rattled with every movement. "I spoke to you," he murmured. "When your mind was weak.

When your soul was cracked. I whispered. I guided. I *entered*.”

My stomach twisted. “Why? Why would you do that?”

His eyes darkened. “Because Maya wouldn’t send you here if she didn’t believe you were broken. If she didn’t believe you were dangerous. Only then would she send you to me. Only then could I see you again.”

“You’re insane,” I gasped.

“I’ was your father,” he said, almost tenderly. “And you were mine.”

I stepped back, my hands shaking. “I’m not like you.”

“No,” he said softly, “you’re stronger.”

The silence that followed felt suffocating.

I needed to know more. I needed to understand.

“Why is this school really here?” I asked, my voice barely a whisper.

He didn’t answer right away. Instead, he walked toward the altar, his movements slow and deliberate. When he finally spoke, his voice was eerily calm.

“The truth will kill you, Arya. Like it did the others.”

“Others?” I whispered.

He nodded, his eyes glinting in the dim light. “Forty students. Each facing their deepest fear during The Hollow Game. Only twenty came back.”

I swallowed hard. “And the others?”

“Demons took them,” he said simply. “Their souls are locked inside the Hollow Rooms. Empty vessels, waiting for the next game.”

I took a step back, the weight of his words crushing me.

And then, Veer’s lips twisted into something like a smile. “You almost didn’t make it. But he helped you.”

“Who?” I gasped, my voice trembling.

Veer's eyes gleamed with something dark. "The devil inside you."

My breath caught in my throat.

The devil inside me?

I wanted to scream, to laugh, to run—but I couldn't move. My body was frozen, my thoughts unraveling like threads from a torn cloth. Veer stood there, unblinking, as if what he said was ordinary. Casual. *Expected.*

"You're lying," I whispered, though it didn't feel true even as I said it.

Veer's expression didn't shift. "Your nightmares… the voice in your head… you always thought it was your fear. But no, Arya. It was me. And him."

"I would've known," I insisted. "I would've felt—"

"You did," he interrupted coldly. "You just called it madness. And madness is the mask the devil wears best."

The air in the prayer hall thickened. The shadows on the walls started to bend unnaturally, like they were listening, breathing. I looked behind me—was the door still open? Had I even closed it?

I took a shaky step back. My fingers grazed the wall. It felt damp. Cold. Like flesh instead of stone.

"I don't want to be part of this," I whispered.

"But you already are," Veer said, and something in his voice turned softer. "You were born into this. You were *prayed* into this. Your mother begged for you. And I... I gave her to the devil."

I felt the blood drain from my face.

"You—what?"

"She doesn't remember. She doesn't want to. She thinks I worshipped darkness alone. But she begged for a child who would never be weak. Never be broken. And I delivered. You are what the devil answered with, Arya. A vessel."

"No," I breathed. "You're insane."

"And yet," he said, walking toward me slowly, "you're standing here… alive, after The Hollow Game… after your soul *should* have been torn apart… but it wasn't, because something inside you fought back harder than even the monsters could."

He stopped, inches away from me. I could smell the metal on his shackles, the rot of old prayers soaked into the altar behind him.

"You're not like the others," he whispered. "You're much, much worse."

I backed away slowly, slipping into the corridor without another word, trying to outrun the silence that seemed to chase me. My feet moved on instinct alone, heart thudding like a war drum in my chest. The hallway twisted, the lights flickering—just like the night I saw the demon on the third bed.

And as I walked back to the hostel, every wall felt closer. Every shadow seemed to whisper.

My father was here.

The devil was inside me.

And the truth?

The truth was just beginning to crack open.

10:THE DEVIL I KNOW

My feet thundered against the cold, cement floor of the corridor. My breath came out in short, ragged bursts, white in the chilly air. Shadows clung to the walls like parasites, whispering in voices too low to hear but too loud to ignore. Veer's words from the dark room still echoed in my skull—strange, cryptic, haunting. His presence had scraped the inside of my bones, left my skin raw. I didn't care if I broke the rules anymore. I just wanted to get away.

I flung open the door to my room and slammed it shut behind me. Elina was already there, sitting cross-legged on her bed, flipping through a worn-out book that looked far too ancient to belong to any girl our age. Her eyes flicked up as if she'd been expecting me all along.

"Elina," I gasped. My voice trembled. "Something's wrong with this place."

She blinked, almost too slowly. "Sit. Tell me."

I collapsed onto my bed, every inch of me shaking. "Veer… he said things. In the dark room. I felt him in my head. He knew things about me… things I've never told anyone. About the incident. The pups. My friends. He —" I choked. "He said *I've always belonged here.*"

A flicker of something passed through her face—pity? No. It was colder than that. Knowing.

I gripped the blanket beneath me. "This school—this hostel—it's not a place for healing, Elina. It's a trap. It's feeding off us. And the third bed…" My voice lowered to a whisper. "I saw something on it. A demon. Crawling. Breathing."

The silence that followed wasn't comforting. It was heavy. Dense. And when Elina finally spoke, her voice no longer carried the same soft sweetness it once did.

"I know."

It was like icewater pouring through my veins.

"What do you mean you *know*?"

Her eyes—once warm and brown—seemed darker now. Ancient. Timeless. "Because I was born here, Arya. A century ago. I've walked these halls longer than you can imagine. I've watched souls come in and never leave. I've watched demons bloom inside children's skins like rot beneath roses."

I reeled. "You're lying."

"I helped bring you here," she said softly, almost like a lullaby. "You were always meant to come. Veer… he made sure of it. And I helped. Because you're not like the others, Arya. You're special. You're the daughter of a devil."

I felt the scream rise up inside me, but it didn't leave my throat. It stayed there like a lump of thorns.

"You were the end of your mother's prayers and the beginning of something far darker. Veer wanted to keep you close. And the warden? She's your blood too. It's in your veins, Arya. Darkness."

I couldn't move. Couldn't breathe. "You're lying," I whispered again, though my soul already knew the truth. It had always known.

Elina stood up and walked toward me, her footsteps soundless. "I was your friend because I wanted to be. But you needed to be here, Arya. You needed to *wake up*."

I backed against the wall. "Then what am I?"

She tilted her head, almost gently. "You're not just the daughter of a devil, Arya. You *are* the devil."

The room seemed to shrink around me. The walls trembled. My heart pounded so violently it hurt. Betrayal throbbed through my chest like a second heartbeat.

I had trusted her. I had clung to her like a rope in the dark. But Elina had been part of the nightmare all along.

And now I was awake.

"No," I whispered. "No, that's not true. You're lying, Elina. You're trying to get into my head just like he did."

Elina smiled, but it wasn't kind. It was the kind of smile that slithered under your skin. "No one's trying, Arya. We've *always* been inside your head. Veer's voice… it never left, did it?"

I wanted to scream. But something else bubbled up first—memories.

I clutched my head as the pain surged through it like a hammer. The dark corners of my mind peeled open like a wound. I remembered the whisper. That same whisper that used to lull me to sleep when I was little. That low voice that called itself my *protector*, my *shadow*, my *friend*. I used to talk to it… at night… when I was scared. And it always answered.

"I was just a child," I murmured, more to myself than her. "Twelve years old…"

Elina tilted her head, watching me unravel. I could barely breathe.

"There was a puppy," I said slowly, trembling. "It followed me home from school. I… I loved it. I kept it in the shed. But then…"

The image tore through me like broken glass.

I saw my small hands soaked in red. I remembered the crunch of bones, the smell of iron. The cries. The laughter—*not mine, no*—his. That voice. That same, low, coaxing voice, whispering inside my mind: *Do it. It's okay. You're special. It won't feel a thing.*

I sobbed, curling into myself. "I thought it was just a nightmare. I thought… I was dreaming."

"You weren't dreaming, Arya," Elina said gently, crouching in front of me. "You were awakening. Veer was guiding you. And you listened, even if you don't remember."

"No…" My voice cracked. "My friends… Annie ,priya."

More flashes. More horror. The school corridor. Their faces. Fear in their eyes. Me, standing over them, covered in blood, holding— *Don't think about it*, my mind screamed. *Don't.*

But I remembered. Oh god, I remembered it all now.

Their screams. My smile. His laughter echoing inside me like a celebration.

I screamed and buried my face in the pillow, my body shaking violently. "Why? Why would he do that? Why me?"

"Because you were born from darkness," Elina said softly. "You are the heir. The bloodline. He needed your mother to send you here. He needed to *find* you."

"I don't remember doing any of it," I sobbed. "I thought I was sick. I thought I needed help. My mother took me to doctors. Psychologists. But no one could explain the things I saw. The voices I heard."

"Because science can't measure what's inside you," Elina replied. "And your mother knew. Deep down, she knew the truth she never dared to say out loud. That you were *never* meant for this world."

I felt hollow. Like my soul had been scooped out and replaced with ice. "She sent me here when I was seventeen," I whispered. "But he… he's been here since I was two."

Elina nodded. "He waited all these years. Shackled. Controlled. But always watching. Always whispering."

My body felt numb. The truth weighed more than any nightmare. "So everything I am… everything I've ever done… it wasn't me?"

"No," Elina said, brushing hair from my face. "It was you, Arya. But it was the *real* you. The part you were too human to accept."

I looked at her with wide, broken eyes. "And you… all this time… you were helping him?"

She nodded. "Because I believe in you. I always have. You're meant for something bigger than this. Something darker. And now, you're finally remembering who you are."

The silence in the room was unbearable. I could hear my heartbeat in my ears. My skin felt too tight for my body. My thoughts, once fragmented, were now whole—and horrifying.

I stared at my reflection in the cracked mirror. Pale. Empty. Lost.

But behind my eyes, something ancient stirred.

Something awake.

11:THE BEGENNING OF END

They say evil is born in silence, in whispers between the dead and the damned. But mine—mine was born in fire. A scream at midnight. A pact sealed in blood. I never needed to learn to be evil. I was born in it. Molded by it. Son of the Devil himself.

The first time I saw Maya, I knew she was too soft for this world. She had eyes like untouched snow and a heart that still believed in light. I never understood what drew me to her—maybe it was the thrill of watching purity rot slowly in my arms. I remember the night we made the pact. The air was thick with incense and secrets. She stood beside me in that broken church, hands trembling as I held the blade to my palm The first time I held Arya, the world stopped breathing.

I remember Maya was asleep from the sedatives, her face pale under the hospital lights. The nurses hesitated to hand her to me at first—I must've looked too wild, too eager. But when they did, when Arya was finally in my arms, it was as if the air shimmered. Her tiny fingers curled around mine, and I felt something ancient stir inside her. Like she had lived this life before. Like she remembered what she was meant to become.

"Look at you," I whispered into her ear, brushing a strand of dark hair off her forehead. "You're everything I asked for. Everything he promised."

I carried her to the window, away from prying eyes. Outside, the sky cracked with thunder. "Even the heavens are jealous," I muttered. "They know who you are now."

Later, when Maya woke up, I was rocking Arya in my arms, humming a lullaby made of forgotten prayers. She flinched.

"What are you singing to her?" she asked sharply.

"Words from the old tongue," I said calmly. "Words she already knows."

"You're scaring me, Veer."

I looked at her then, my eyes empty of softness. "You should be."

—

The days that followed were strange and sacred.

I used to take Arya into the attic late at night when Maya was asleep. I'd place candles around her crib, draw ancient sigils on the floor. I'd hold her hands and whisper, "One day, you'll understand. One day, you'll thank me."

One night, she looked straight at the flickering flame and giggled. "Dada," she said. Her first word. Not "Mama." *Dada*. My heart clenched like it was being carved open.

"She knows me," I said aloud. "She remembers."

—

But Maya ruined everything.

"You're filling her head with poison!" she yelled one morning, snatching Arya from my arms. "She's a baby, not your weapon."

"She's not a baby," I said coldly. "She's a flame in disguise."

"She's *mine*, Veer!"

"No," I stepped forward, voice low. "She's *ours*. But she's *his*, more than anything. She belongs to the blood."

"You're sick," Maya whispered, tears running down her face. "You're obsessed."

I didn't deny it.

One night, after a brutal fight, I found Arya asleep in her crib, her lips parted, cheeks red from crying. I sat beside her, touched her forehead with shaking fingers.

"You're everything," I murmured. "I would burn the world to see you smile. I would slit the sun's throat if it ever made you cry."

Sometimes I'd find Maya watching us, silent horror in her eyes. She saw the way I looked at Arya. Like she was divine. Untouchable. *Mine.*

"You're not in love with her, Veer," Maya hissed once. "You're *possessed* by her."

I smiled then, slow and unblinking. "Exactly."

—

The last night, it all came to an end.

We fought like animals. Glass shattered. Blood spilled. Arya stood at the stairs, clinging to her stuffed crow, eyes wide but not frightened.

"You're not taking her from me!" I roared.

"She's not safe with you!" Maya sobbed. "You'll ruin her!"

"She was never *meant* to be safe, Maya! She was meant to be *glorious!*"

And then I snapped. I don't remember how the knife got in my hand. Don't remember slicing Maya's arm or dragging her to the wall. But I do remember Arya's voice, so small, so calm.

"Papa."

I turned. She was watching. Not crying. Not scared. Watching.

"I love you," she said.

I dropped the knife.

Minutes later, the police arrived.

And as they dragged me away in chains, Maya shaking behind them, Arya stood by the window, pressing her palm to the glass.

"I'll come for you," I whispered through bloodied lips. "I'll take you away. I promise."

—

I did.

Seventeen years later, she came.

But the world has changed now.

And this time... she's going to remember everything.

They thought separating us would end everything.

But blood doesn't break with handcuffs.

The devil inside me knew that once a connection was made—it couldn't be undone. I *was* her father. I *was* her creator. But more than anything, I was the *voice* in her head. And they couldn't shackle that.

Even inside those concrete walls they called a prison, I found her. Through dreams, through shadows, through her own innocent fears—I slipped into her thoughts like poison into water. Gently. Slowly. Completely.

When Arya was seven, I sent her a nightmare. A simple one—our old attic, the sigils on the floor glowing red, her toys whispering her name. She woke up screaming, clutching at nothing. Maya told herself it was just night terrors. Foolish woman.

At nine, I planted a suggestion. Just a whisper while she slept.

"The dogs bark too much. They know too much. Make it stop."

The next morning, three neighborhood puppies were found drowned in the well. Arya had no memory of it. Maya cried for weeks. I smiled through my prison bars.

When she was twelve... I got bold.

I slipped in deeper. Not just whispers—but *commands*. I called to the seed of darkness already inside her. The one that never fully closed its eyes. I told it to wake up.

Her classmates used to mock her—call her strange, haunted, silent. They had no idea how right they were. One day, during art class, she found a rusted pair of scissors under her desk. I remember her staring at them like they were alive. She took them home that day. That night, I whispered again.

"Make them stop laughing. Paint with red."

Two of her closest friends were found slashed, hidden under the oak tree at school. No one could prove it. No one even suspected Arya.

But Maya did.

She knew. She always knew.

She packed Arya's bags and dragged her to the church-school, the one hidden behind the veil of purity and salvation. She thought it was safe. Thought she was hiding Arya from *me*.

But she sent her straight into my arms.

Because this wasn't just a school.

It was *ours*.

My mother—Arya's grandmother—had been waiting here. She and I created this place as a feeding ground. A slaughterhouse for wandering souls. Every child that stepped inside thought they were escaping something.

They didn't know they were walking into Hell.

But Arya... she was different.

She was born of Hell.

I remember the first day she stepped through the gate.

I stood at the window of the boy's dorm, shackled at the ankles, trembling like a creature seeing the sun for the first time. She looked just like Maya—but her eyes... her eyes were mine.

"I told you, baby," I whispered to the wind. "I'd come for you. And now... you're here."

From then on, I kept feeding her mind, gently opening the buried memories. The blood, the scissors, the whispers in the attic. I watched her flinch every time she passed a mirror. Because deep down, some part of her *remembered.*

She's breaking now. Slowly.

But beautifully.

And when she finally accepts what she is... when she stops running from the monster in her blood...

She'll become everything I ever dreamed of.

My little girl.

The Devil's daughter.

Born to burn the world.

12:THE GATHERING SOULS

I didn't mean to end up here.

All I wanted was to escape—to run as far away from these walls, these rules, these people. My heart had been pounding ever since I'd begun seeing things—rooms full of red-eyed shadows, the corridors pulsing like a living thing, doors whispering my name. Every step I took only led me deeper, and now… I was trapped. Again.

The room was circular, like some ritual hall, its walls made of black stone that breathed with the agony of something ancient. No windows. No door that I could remember walking through. The air was cold, but I was burning from the inside out.

And then I saw them.

Three figures.

Veer. Elina. And the Warden.

They were waiting for me.

I froze. My legs felt like they belonged to someone else. My throat closed with panic. My hands wouldn't stop shaking. Veer's smile was carved from something inhuman. Elina stood tall, her eyes glistening with a manic pride. And the Warden—her silence was worse than screams.

I took a step back, but the wall behind me was warm. Alive.

"You've come," Veer said softly. "We were hoping you'd stop pretending."

My lips parted. I couldn't speak. My heartbeat echoed in my ears.

"Why am I here?" I managed to whisper.

"To remember," the Warden said, stepping closer. "To accept."

Veer tilted his head, eyes gleaming. "To finally know who you are."

I shook my head. "I *know* who I am. You people—you're monsters—"

"No," Elina cut me off. "You're family."

That word. *Family.* It struck something deep and hollow inside me.

The Warden's voice broke through the cold silence. "Do you know who I am?"

I swallowed, my chest rising and falling like I was drowning. I looked at her. Her eyes. Her jaw. Her voice. Something… something was familiar. Too familiar.

"No," I lied.

She stepped forward, her hand touching my cheek. I didn't move.

"I'm your grandmother."

My heart stopped.

Something in me cracked. I couldn't breathe.

"You're lying," I said, stepping back. "You're lying—this is all some sick—"

"No," Veer said. "This is your blood, Arya. We are your blood."

And then they told me everything.

About the prayer made to the devil. About my mother's desperation. About Veer—his bloodline—his mother who owned this hostel, this cage dressed as a school. They told me about the souls trapped here, about the demons, about the darkness fed to us daily in the name of healing.

"You were born from darkness," Elina said, stepping forward. "You're his gift."

My legs gave out, and I dropped to the floor. I saw flashes—Veer's face hovering over me when I was just a baby. Him whispering in my mind. His voice that sounded like my own thoughts. The times I killed. The blood on my hands. The puppies. My friends. The laughing, then screaming.

It wasn't me.

But it was inside me.

"I'm not like you," I breathed, eyes wide. "I'm not evil."

Veer knelt beside me, brushing a lock of hair from my face. "You're not evil, Arya. You're *pure*. Uncompromised. That's why we need you."

Elina knelt on my other side, her hand on my shoulder. "You've already done more than most ever could. You've tasted blood. Now learn to control it."

I looked at all of them. Their eyes. Their sick devotion. Their hunger.

My body trembled. But my mind… it went still.

This was it.

If I didn't play their game, I'd never get out of here. I'd never find the truth. I'd never destroy the thing growing inside me.

So I nodded.

Slowly. Deliberately.

"I understand," I whispered.

Veer's smile stretched wide.

The Warden exhaled. Elina smiled like she'd been waiting for this her whole life.

But deep inside, buried beneath layers of fear, rage, and broken memories… I made a promise to myself.

I will burn this place to the ground.

But first, I'll become one of them.

And they'll never see it coming.

I walked the corridor like I'd done a hundred times before—but this time, I wasn't Arya, the student. I was Arya, the monster. Arya, the cursed daughter. Arya, the truth-seeker.

My steps echoed across the cold stone floor, bouncing off hollow walls that no longer whispered, but screamed. I clutched the banister tighter as I descended into the dim hallway beneath the main building. The walls wept moisture. The silence hummed.

I needed answers.

"Where are they?" I asked Elina, the moment she appeared behind me without a sound.

She smiled. "Who, darling? The students?"

My heart twisted.

"Yes. I've seen them. Laughed with them. Slept beside them. You—you can't tell me they're not real."

She tilted her head. "And yet, they were never truly *there*."

My blood froze. My legs numbed. I stared at her, words lodging in my throat.

"It was all for you," a second voice added, calm and venomous—Veer, stepping forward from the shadows like he belonged to them. "Every room, every face, every scream. Just for you, Arya. To make you *see*."

I stumbled back. My spine hit the wall, hard. "What do you mean? What do you *mean*?!"

The warden appeared last, walking with the stillness of a corpse. She didn't speak at first—her eyes did. They were old. Older than time itself. She moved like a memory. A haunting.

"You were never supposed to see them as humans," she said. "They were shapes. Echoes. Demons wrapped in skin. Every girl and boy you met here, they were just shadows of your mind. Crafted carefully, with just enough humanity to feel... real."

"Why?" My voice cracked like old wood.

"To test you," Veer said.

"To trap you," Elina whispered.

"To break you," the warden concluded.

"No," I shook my head, tears starting to fall, "No. You're lying. I touched them. I fought them. I slept in the same room. I heard their breathing. I saw them die!"

Elina's laugh was soft and cruel. "You heard what we let you hear. You saw what we *needed* you to see. Every death, every game... they were rituals, Arya. Doors we opened inside you."

I dropped to my knees.

Veer walked closer and crouched beside me, his voice gentle, fatherly. "You always believed you were surrounded by others. That this place was some kind of hell for misfits, right? That was easier for your mind to handle. But the truth is much worse..."

He leaned into my ear.

"This hostel is a prison, yes. But you were never just a prisoner."

My breath hitched.

"You were the reason it was built."

The silence stretched. Then the warden spoke, her voice a grave being unearthed.

"Forty rooms. Forty doors. Twenty devils locked inside the walls. Twenty others consumed. All for you."

I looked up slowly. "And Mr. Yusuf?"

Elina chuckled. "Oh, sweet child. You still think he was real?"

I screamed. A raw, inhuman sound. The hallway shook. My skin felt like it was peeling from the inside.

"You made me kill," I said, sobbing now, "You made me do those things when I was a child. I thought I was insane—I thought I was broken."

"You were never broken," Veer said, gently stroking my hair.

"You were born whole."

The world tilted.

I felt the walls close in again. But this time, I didn't run. I stood.

My hands trembled. My breath came sharp.

And deep inside... behind the fear, behind the sorrow... something stirred.

Something dark.

But I clung to the last bit of light.

I *had* to.

13:THE ILLUSION OF FLESH

The corridor was too quiet.

Too quiet.

I could hear my own breath. My own heartbeat. The tick of the clock on the hallway wall—yet there was no clock. Just that ticking sound crawling down my spine like wet fingertips. I walked, barefoot and silent, across the cold floor of the hostel, every step heavier than the last. I wasn't running this time. I wasn't hiding. I had decided to *stay*.

To play along. To become what they wanted.

That's how I'd escape.

But as the echo of my steps faded, replaced by whispers in the walls—whispers that sounded like my name—I realized something: I didn't even know who "they" were anymore.

I opened the door to my dorm room slowly. The third bed was still there.

Always made. Always untouched. Always... watching.

And tonight, I was going to lie in it.

"Finally," Veer's voice echoed behind me.

I turned, but he was already inside. His tall figure blocking the door, shackled ankles dragging softly like metal whispers on the tile. The chains were part of him now—like they'd grown out of his skin. He smiled. Not like a father. Not like a classmate. Something in between. Something far more *inhuman*.

"You're early," I said coldly.

"I knew you'd come." He walked toward the third bed and tapped the pillow gently. "You always belonged here. You just didn't know it yet."

I stayed standing.

"What is this place?" I asked. "Really. I want the truth now."

The silence that followed wasn't empty. It was *full*. Full of laughter, screaming, chanting. The room spun even though I stood still.

Then came the warden. She appeared at the door like a shadow with bones, wrapped in silence and that permanent smirk she wore. Elena followed, leaning against the doorframe, arms crossed, her eyes glowing like molten glass.

"You want the truth?" the Warden said, stepping in. Her voice was dry, ancient. Familiar. "Then sit down, Arya. It's time you understood what you were born into."

I didn't sit. But I didn't leave either.

"I saw them," I whispered. "The students. The classes. The games. Were they all fake?"

"No," Elena replied. "They were very real—*to you*. Illusions. Designed to break you. Twist your soul. The hostel was always empty. You just didn't see the truth… because you weren't ready."

"And now I am?"

"Now," Veer interrupted, stepping forward, "you're *awakening*. Your soul was too human, too fragile. So I… helped."

I flinched. My mind splintered.

"You…" My voice cracked. "You were the one in my head. When I was twelve… You told me to kill them."

"Yes," he said softly, like it was a lullaby. "Because it was the only way to get you here. Your mother wouldn't send you unless she feared you. So I gave her a reason."

I couldn't breathe.

"The puppies… my best friends—"

"They were never your friends, Arya," Veer snarled. "They were obstacles. Noise. But now look at you. You've made it home."

The third bed loomed behind me like an open grave.

I took a step back.

"And the voice that haunted me?" I asked. "The whispers at night? The cold hands? That wasn't me?"

"No," the Warden said. "That was *him*, channeling himself through the link he shares with you. Blood calls to blood."

"And the third bed," I whispered, unable to turn around. "Whose was it?"

Veer's smile turned wicked. "Yours."

"What?"

"It's not for the *human* Arya. It's for the part of you that belongs to *us*. The part we were always trying to wake up."

I turned.

The bed no longer looked empty.

A girl sat there now. Same black hair. Same face. Same wide, broken eyes.

Me.

But not *me*.

She smiled—vicious and hollow.

"You can join me now," she said, her voice stitched with mine, her lips curling. "You don't have to fight anymore. The devil doesn't want your soul, Arya. He already owns it."

My knees gave in.

I dropped beside the bed, gasping for breath. I wasn't sure if I was still awake. Still alive. Still... Arya.

"You played with me," I said to Veer, tears spilling. "All my life. You were never a father. You were a monster."

"I *am* your father," he said, kneeling. "And monsters raise monsters. That's the rule."

"No," I hissed, trembling. "My mother—"

"Is gone," the Warden snapped. "She gave up. She lost. And you—" she knelt beside me now, "—you have something she never did. *Power.* We just want to help you use it."

"Why me?" I whispered.

"Because you were born of *hell,*" Veer said gently. "And *nobody knows* what hell looks like... until it stares back from your own reflection."

I looked up.

The third-bed Arya was smiling wider now.

So I did what I knew I had to.

I smiled back

I didn't want to smile.

But I did.

Because in that moment, I knew I was no longer allowed to cry.

The third-bed Arya—my shadow, my reflection, my curse—reached out her hand like we were sisters reunited after centuries. And the worst part? It didn't feel foreign. It felt like a homecoming.

My fingers twitched, almost reaching out to touch her. Her skin looked like mine, but wrong—too smooth, too cold, too dead.

I blinked and she was gone.

The bed was made again. Neat. Clean. Untouched.

But now I knew the truth.

That bed had always been mine.

It was the place where my nightmares crawled out from. Where my real self whispered in my ear, feeding me screams. It was the mirror I refused to look into—and now, they had shoved it in my face.

"You see it now, don't you?" Elena said from behind me. "The duality. The war inside your own bones. One half of you wants to run. The other... just wants to *burn* everything."

Veer stepped closer, his voice lower, more intimate. "Do you remember that night, Arya? When you tore apart your classmate's face with a pencil?"

My breath caught.

I hadn't remembered that in years.

"You were twelve. She laughed at you. And then… I spoke to you. I told you what to do. And you *listened*. Do you remember the warmth in your hands afterward?"

"Stop..." I whispered.

"You liked it," he said. "The way the blood smeared like paint. The way she screamed your name. You liked being seen."

"Stop it."

"She *saw* you, Arya. The real you. And that scared you more than anything."

"I SAID STOP!"

I screamed so loud I thought my lungs would tear.

And yet they all just stared. Calm. Waiting.

The warden walked forward now. Slowly. Not like a woman, but like a creature that had worn the shape of one for too long.

She crouched beside me and took my chin in her cold, bony hand.

She tilted her head. "I raised your father. I watched him rot from the inside out, begging for your mother's love. And when she ran, I told him to wait. Wait until his daughter was old enough to carry what he couldn't."

"You made him into this," I whispered.

"No," she said, almost kindly. "The devil made *us*. And now we've made *you*."

The room began to warp. The walls bled with shadows. The lights flickered—not electrical, but spiritual. Like the room was breathing.

"I don't want this," I said.

"But you were born for it," Elena cut in. "We *all* heard the whispers the night you were born. The devil himself lit the sky red. You were chosen before you took your first breath."

"You don't get to decide who I am," I spat.

Veer crouched beside me again, eyes soft. "You already decided. When you killed. When you laughed after. When you looked at your own hands and didn't regret it."

My voice trembled. "That was you... you *made* me do it."

He shrugged. "I only unlocked what was already there."

I stood up. Slowly. Carefully.

"Then maybe I can lock it back."

Their eyes narrowed. They didn't like that.

"Don't pretend you're one of *them*," Elena sneered. "You've *tasted* what it feels like to be one of us. Don't lie to yourself, Arya."

"I'm not lying," I said. "I'm *choosing*. There's a difference."

Veer moved forward so fast I didn't see the motion—only the result. His face inches from mine, his breath warm and terrifying.

"You'll come around," he whispered. "You'll sleep in that bed tonight. And when you do, she'll crawl back into you. And you won't push her away this time."

My jaw clenched.

"What if I do sleep in it?" I asked, faking surrender. "What happens then?"

He smiled. "You wake up as yourself."

And so I nodded.

I turned to the bed.

I peeled back the covers. Slowly. Reverently.

Like I was opening the gate to my own grave.

I lay down.

The bed was cold at first… but then it wrapped around me like hands. Like a hundred arms of smoke, pulling me in.

I didn't scream.

I closed my eyes.

And I smiled.

Because **they thought I was giving in**.

But in my heart, in the silence only I could hear—**my mother's voice still lived.** A soft hum. A warmth. A truth.

14:I AM NOT ALONE

They watched me. Every step I took, every breath I exhaled, their eyes followed like hounds ready to snap the moment I slipped. Veer stood silently, almost proud, his smirk carved like a scar across his face. Elina, poised with elegance, her eyes gleaming with a satisfaction that churned my stomach. And the Warden—my grandmother, though I hadn't dared to say it aloud—hovered like a shadow from my nightmares, her presence heavy, suffocating.

I had to become them to destroy them. I had to burn with their fire, even if it scorched my soul in the process.

"She's ready," Veer said, watching me from the corner of the cold hall. *"I can feel it. The devil's blood has finally awoken."* I smiled—a smile I had rehearsed in the mirror of my mind a thousand times. Cold. Void. Inhuman.

"Yes," I whispered. "It feels… right."

But inside?

It felt like rot. Like I was digging a grave with my own hands.

They led me into the rituals. The chamber where blood was memory and fire was truth. They handed me the blade—a symbolic one, they said— and told me to recite the vows that tied my soul to the family of devils. I spoke every word as if I believed them, while my insides screamed.

"You will learn to destroy without mercy," the Warden chanted.

"I will," I replied, each syllable tasting like ash.

"You will drown the world in the storm that runs in your veins," Elina echoed.

"I was born for it," I said with a smile I had to staple to my face.

But when they turned away, I clenched my fists so tight I felt my nails cut skin. I stared at the blood and thought, *this is not mine. This is not who I am.*

At night, I returned to the room.

The **third bed** welcomed me now—like it had waited all these years. But the truth was no longer running from me.

That bed was *mine*. Not for the Arya who once laughed, who loved books and counted stars.

But for the darkness Veer had stitched into my bones.

"Sleep well," he had whispered once through the walls, when I was twelve. *"I'll take care of the rest."*

And he did. He took my hands. My eyes. My innocence. He made me **hurt**. Made me kill.

I remembered the blood of the puppies on my shoes. The glassy eyes of my best friend as her body stopped shaking.

I didn't remember *doing* it, but I remembered the voice.

"They were never your friends, Arya. You were just cleansing the dirt."

My fists shook against the sheets now. The room had gone cold.

And then… the whispers came.

But not Veer's.

Not this time.

These were different. Faint echoes, soft voices—children, teens, girls, boys—*souls*. The lost ones. The ones this family had consumed.

"You are not one of them..." one whispered.

"We know what you are trying to do."

"We want to help you, Arya."

Tears burned the corners of my eyes. I couldn't breathe. I wasn't alone.
Not anymore.

The next morning, I set the room on fire.

Not with flames—but with performance.

I walked into the hall in black. My eyes rimmed with charcoal, the way they taught me. I didn't blink as the Warden spoke of torment. I didn't flinch when Veer tested me—handing me a live crow and asking me to snap its neck.

I did it.

But inside, I screamed.

"She's one of us now," Elina whispered.

"She's perfect," the Warden declared.

Veer didn't say a word.

He only watched.

Maybe he knew.

Maybe he could feel the war inside me—the storm that wasn't just evil, but *righteous* fury. I was coming for them.

And they didn't even see it

The air in the hostel had changed. Or maybe… I had. The floor felt colder beneath my bare feet. The silence held more voices than ever. Even the walls—those suffocating, ancient walls—seemed to whisper. As if they *knew* the truth I was hiding behind my smile.

"Why do you walk like that now?" Elina asked one evening, tilting her head like a crow observing a dying animal.

I turned to her slowly. "Like what?"

"Like you belong here."

I met her gaze with something unreadable—something I had stolen from the dead faces I'd seen in my dreams. "Maybe I always did."

She smiled. But I could tell she wasn't sure anymore. Good. Let them question. Let them fear. Let them believe I was their prodigy while I crafted their destruction in silence.

That night, I returned to the corridor. The one lined with rusted doors and whispers leaking from behind them. I walked past each door slowly— touching the handles, feeling their chill. They weren't locked anymore.

Something had changed.

Or *someone* had unlocked them.

"Hello?" I whispered.

The corridor answered.

"You were never supposed to end like this."

"You still have time."

"The fire in your blood is not theirs to own."

The voices... they were like wind—quiet, but furious. Like screams wrapped in blankets, begging to be heard. I leaned against the cold stone wall and let the tears come. Silently. Quietly. I hadn't cried in years. Not after mother left me. Not after the hostel swallowed me whole.

But tonight… the silence allowed it.

The next morning, Veer called me into the sanctuary. That's what they called the underground chamber that smelled of burnt metal and ash. Where rituals lived. Where devils were fed.

He stood there, waiting with two candles and a blade.

"Elina says you've been wandering," he said.

I stayed silent.

"She says the voices follow you now."

Still silent.

Veer stepped closer. His chains clinked faintly. Even now—**after all these years—he remained shackled at the ankles**. They said it was for safety.

But I knew.

It was because even the devils feared him.

"I heard you speaking to the walls," he said, almost gently. "Are they telling you the truth? Or lies?"

"I don't know," I whispered.

He smiled, slowly. "Good. That means you're awakening."

He handed me the blade.

"Prove it."

There was a bird in the cage again. Another poor thing trembling, feathers broken. He wanted me to kill it. Again.

I stared at it.

I wanted to scream. To tear my skin apart. To claw my heart out just to make it stop beating with their rhythm.

But I raised the blade.

And I did it.

The bird didn't cry. I did.

Inside. Quietly.

Later that night, I curled into the third bed. My bed. The bed for the devil's daughter.

But it wasn't the bed that haunted me anymore.

It was what I remembered.

When I was younger, the spirit had come to me. A dark silhouette at night. Breathing cold air into my mouth. Whispering things into my ears. I had thought it was a ghost. An evil soul.

But now I knew.

That voice, that breath—it was *me*. It was the darkness inside me. Or worse—it was Veer, inside my mind.

"Kill her, Arya. She laughed at you."

"They're not your friends."

"You were born to rule them, not live among them."

Those weren't dreams.

They were instructions.

And now, they wanted me to become that voice.

To whisper to others. To take what Veer gave me and pass it forward like a poisoned gift.

But I wouldn't.

I couldn't.

Because every time I looked into the eyes of my supposed "family," I remembered something else.

My mother's eyes.

Soft. Human. Full of stories. She had sent me here out of fear—but also hope. She had believed there was still good in me. That the evil could be undone.

And she was right.

Because that good, no matter how deeply buried, was still there.

And it was furious.

The next day, I watched Elina take a child—one of the illusions, a small boy who barely spoke—and vanish with him into the west wing.

I followed. Quietly. Careful not to let my heart race too loudly.

I didn't find them. But I found the blood.

On the wall. On the floor. On a single white shoe that lay abandoned by the door.

They weren't just illusions.

They were sacrifices.

And the family I was pretending to be part of… they were monsters.

But they didn't know me. Not really.

I wasn't one of them.

Not truly.

I was *something else.*

And when I rose, it wouldn't be with chains or blades.

It would be with every soul they had buried screaming at my back.

15:BETRAYAL

The silence had begun to feel louder than screams. The walls of the hostel seemed to breathe with me now—exhaling darkness, inhaling deception. I had become the perfect devil's daughter. At least, that's what they believed.

I walked through the hallway that once made me tremble. Now I walked it barefoot, calm, with a smile that didn't touch my soul. My hands were still sticky from the crimson act Veer had asked me to perform—another "ritual" to prove myself. I had carved symbols into a table with a knife while chanting words I didn't understand, but they tasted like rust and rot in my mouth. I had done worse. I had *pretended* to enjoy it.

Every time Veer looked at me with that twisted sense of pride, I wanted to scream. Every time the Warden patted my back, whispering how I had her blood in my veins, I wanted to rip it out. And Elina...she watched me too closely, her smile sharp, eyes hollow. As if she was waiting for my mask to slip.

But it wouldn't. Not yet.

Because now, the dead were speaking to me.

It started as a breeze. Soft. Cold. A whisper brushing past my ear when I walked into the prayer room where they made me kneel in front of the devil's symbol.

"She poisoned the children in the kitchen."

I froze.

Elina was standing behind me. I turned to see if she had said something, but she only nodded with approval at my kneeling form. I bowed again, heart pounding.

Later that night, when I lay on the third bed, the one that used to terrify me, a voice emerged from beneath the floorboards.

"She feeds off fear. She once drowned a girl for smiling."

It didn't say who. But I *knew* it was the Warden.

These weren't hallucinations.

They were secrets. The souls—they were watching me. Whispering. Stirring.

The next morning, I was taken to the courtyard. A dead tree stood at the center, blackened bark twisted like screaming faces. Veer handed me a small bird in a cage.

"Break its neck," he said, with the calm of a man offering tea.

I held the bird. It was warm. Breathing.

"Elina did this once," Veer added. "She was just six."

I stared at the bird. It blinked at me.

I closed my fist around its body, eyes burning with unshed tears. *Don't feel. Don't break now.* I snapped its neck.

They applauded.

But in my head—another whisper.

"He set the nursery on fire. They were infants."

I didn't ask who.

I *knew*.

I started hearing them more often now.

In reflections—smudges forming faces behind me.

In dreams—children reaching out from the fire.

"Behind the library wall." "The basement isn't just storage." "The chains in Veer's room are for you."

I wrote every word in a book I hid beneath the third bed—my bed— where I no longer feared the evil presence. Because I knew now, it was me. But I also knew the *real* evil was outside of me. Walking. Talking. Loving me in the name of darkness.

So I smiled more. I laughed when Elina cracked jokes about the last girl who tried to escape.

I stood with the Warden and helped her chant spells in blood.

I let Veer touch my face and say, "My daughter. Finally home."

And I said, "Yes, father."

But every time I said it, I felt more hate. More fire.

They thought they had turned me into a devil.

But I was becoming something else.

I was becoming a storm

It began with the mirror.

I saw it flicker when I passed. My reflection blinked a second too late. The eyes in the glass weren't mine. They were hollow, full of fire and fog. I stared at it for a long time until the breath fogged it over and, written in the mist, appeared four shaking words:

"Do not trust them."

I turned. No one was there. But I felt something. Watching me.

That night, the wind outside didn't sound like wind. It sounded like… voices. Screams pressed into whispers. Begging. Crying. And then, laughing.

I laid in the third bed—my bed now—staring at the cracked ceiling above me when something cold touched my ankle.

I looked down.

There was a *hand*.

Bone-thin. Skin melted like wax. Long fingers coiled around my foot and yanked.

Before I could scream, I was pulled *beneath* the bed.

There was nothing but darkness down there. No floor. No end. Just... darkness and silence and *them*.

Eyes opened around me—dozens. Hundreds. Pale and glowing. Some red, some blue, all dead.

A girl floated towards me, skin translucent, eyes hollowed out. Her mouth opened unnaturally wide, and yet her voice was soft:

"You took my place."

Another one—half her jaw missing—came closer, whispering in a voice that sounded like blades on glass:

"We were like you… until they fed on us."

I tried to crawl backward, but more arms wrapped around me. Not hurting. Just *holding* me.

"Listen, Arya." "They won't let you leave." "Veer poisoned me in my sleep." "The Warden made us drink it." "Elina smiled while I died."

Each ghost carried a memory, and as they touched me, those memories bled into my mind. Screams. Needles. Fires. Chains. Laughter. *So much laughter.*

I clutched my head.

"Stop it!" I cried.

But they didn't stop.

One of them, a boy with a stitched throat, leaned close and whispered, **"You have to end it. Only you can."**

When I woke, I was still under the bed.

But it wasn't just a space anymore. It had transformed. A circular room. Stone walls. Black roots crawling like veins. Candles floated in midair, and behind each one stood a child. Dead. Burned. Broken. Some were missing limbs. Others… faces.

But all of them were looking at *me*.

A girl with a burnt smile stepped forward. Her dress dripped blood like rain.

"We are the forgotten. You are our storm." "But they think you are theirs." "Prove them wrong."

She reached out, offering me a blade—not metal. Bone. Carved from something… human.

"There's a room behind the library," she said. "They keep the real records there." "Find it. Before they find *you*."

Another voice followed:

"When the time comes… light the church on fire. That's where they feed."

I emerged from under the bed gasping, body cold, soaked in sweat. My door was wide open. And the Warden stood there.

"Nightmares again?" she asked sweetly.

I forced a nod. "They're getting clearer," I whispered.

She smiled like a mother. "Good. That means the evil in you is waking up."

But what she didn't know was—so were the dead.

Elina entered the room like she belonged in the shadows—graceful, silent, and dangerous. Her dark eyes scanned me, and something about the way she smiled made my spine crawl.

"Good morning, dearest Arya," she said, her voice laced with syrup and venom.

Veer didn't respond to her. Neither did the Warden. There was a heavy silence between the three of them—as if they all knew something I wasn't ready to learn yet.

I didn't speak either. I just stared at the empty plate in front of me.

The breakfast was simple. Toasted bread. Half-cooked eggs. A black liquid they called coffee but tasted like burned blood. I chewed quietly, every bite making my throat tighten.

They all watched me eat.

"Isn't it nice?" Elina murmured, tearing a piece of her toast delicately. "A family breakfast. Just like old times."

Old times? My fingers froze over the crust. My mind was screaming again, a thousand questions pressing against my skull, but I stayed still. Calm. Evil girls don't shake. Evil girls don't cry.

I smiled faintly and nodded. "It's perfect."

Veer smirked. Elina raised her glass. The Warden didn't touch her food. She only watched me with those silver-grey eyes like she was trying to crawl inside my soul.

After the last sip of that wretched coffee, I excused myself quietly and slipped into the bathroom.

The moment the door closed behind me, I exhaled—my spine loosening like I'd been holding in breath for hours.

Steam rose as I turned the old tap. The bathroom was massive—carved from stone, stained by time. The mirror was cracked. The tiles were slick with mildew.

As the water ran, I stared at myself.

There was blood beneath my fingernails.

Not from today.

Not even from yesterday.

I didn't even remember whose it was.

I slipped out of my clothes and stepped under the water, letting it scorch my skin. I needed to feel something. I needed to *burn* this fear off me.

But something shifted behind me.

A shadow. Barely there.

I spun around.

Nothing.

Just the mirror fogging up. The slow drip of water.

Then the lights flickered.

Once.

Twice.

And then—gone.

Darkness swallowed the room whole.

I blinked, hands gripping the edge of the wall.

"It's just the power. Just the power."

But then I felt it.

Hands.

Ice-cold fingers around my ankle.

I shrieked and slipped, hitting the floor hard, my body slamming against wet stone.

Then another hand.

And another.

From beneath the tub.

From inside the *walls*.

They're here.

I tried to crawl away, but they dragged me—*pulled* me like I weighed nothing.

My nails scratched the floor, but it made no sound. The bathroom was silent except for my breath and the *whispers.*

"Arya…" "Finally…" "Come see what they hid…" "You were never one of them…"

I screamed, but water poured into my mouth. Not from above.

From *beneath* me.

As if the tiles had turned to liquid.

They dragged me down. Into the floor. Into the third layer of hell beneath this cursed hostel.

I kicked and flailed, but it was like swimming through oil. Slippery, suffocating.

Then—darkness. And silence.

When I opened my eyes again, I was no longer in the bathroom.

I was in that same old hallway. The one that didn't exist in maps. The one with walls that bled. The one with the **door that breathed.**

Only this time—I didn't walk here.

The spirits brought me.

And they weren't kind anymore.

Their faces were half-melted. Limbs twisted. Some crawled. Some floated. One sobbed without a mouth.

But they *all* looked at me now.

No longer illusions. No longer silent.

"Arya," one whispered. "You have to remember."

"You *saw* us," another hissed. "You walked past our graves every day."

"You were born to be one of *them*, but you chose *this*."

I backed away.

"What are you talking about?" I asked, my voice breaking. "Why me? What do you *want* from me?"

A little boy—burned, his arms missing—crawled toward me and pointed at my chest.

"You hold the key. *You* are the crack in their perfect prison."

"They're scared of you," a faceless girl said. "That's why they want you to become *one of them*."

Suddenly, a door behind me slammed open.
The third bed.
My bed.
Covered in chains and candle wax. The sheets were stitched with veins. The pillow bled ink.

"Lie in it," one spirit whispered.

"See who you *really are*."

"Face what he made you forget."

And then… I saw *her*.
The version of me that used to haunt my dreams.
Standing by the bed.
Wearing my face.
Smiling.

"Come sleep, Arya," she said. "We have so much *to remember*."

16:SCREAMS

The cold metal of the bathtub hugged my skin, and for once, the silence didn't feel safe—it felt *watched*. I could hear the water drip, drip, drip from the rusted faucet, but under that… something else. Breathing. Ragged, shallow breathing. *Not mine.*

I sat up slowly. Fog curled over the mirror, but the letters that appeared this time weren't written by my finger.

"Remember us."

A whisper clawed against the back of my skull. A voice, guttural and cracked, *"She won't let you leave… unless we do."*

I stood, skin prickling, heart hammering. I wrapped the towel around myself, trembling not from cold but from the *presence*. The floorboards creaked behind me. I turned—nothing. But the shadow across the wall was no longer mine. It had *horns*.

Suddenly, I felt it—icy hands gripping my ankles. I screamed, tried to move, but the tiles beneath me gave way. Cracked open like brittle bones. I fell.

Down.

Down.

Into darkness.

The bathtub vanished, and I was falling through black tar, thick and suffocating. Whispers filled the void:

"She drowned us."

"He burned us."

"They laughed while we screamed."

And then—

The third bed.

I landed hard. There it was. A single bed in a room with no walls. No ceiling. Just darkness and that **bed**. Covered in scratch marks and dried blood. Chains hung from each post.

And curled on the mattress… was *me*.

Or rather, what I *could* have been.

Her eyes were red. Her skin pale and stretched, twitching like she'd been starved. She smiled when she saw me.

"Finally," she hissed. *"We meet, Arya."*

I backed away. "You're not real."

She giggled, unnatural and slow, *"Oh, but I am. You were just pretending not to see me. But I've been with you since you were twelve. When you killed those puppies? When that boy fell from the rooftop? You didn't slip. I pushed you."*

My knees buckled. I couldn't breathe. "No… that was Veer. That voice was Veer's!"

She tilted her head. *"It started as Veer. But I grew from him. Your darkness birthed me. And now… I'm ready."*

Chains slithered like snakes. I tried to run, but ghostly hands emerged from the floor—dozens—grabbing my wrists, my ankles, my throat.

They whispered their truths:

"Elina was the one who made us drink it…"

"The Warden watched while the fire burned our dorms."

"Veer… Veer laughed when he fed my sister to the well."

The water from the showerhead was barely warm, trailing down my spine in thin, hesitant drops. My fingers traced the scars that hadn't been there yesterday—burned, clawed, etched by something unseen. My reflection in the cracked bathroom mirror blinked slower than I did.

I leaned in.

The mirror didn't show steam anymore. It showed frost.

Then it shattered.

A cold gust swept the bathroom, slamming the door shut behind me.

I spun, heart pounding—but there was no one. Only silence. Silence that pulsed.

Then I heard them.

Faint at first. Like wind whimpering through a grave.

Then clearer.

Children.

Dozens of them.

Their voices curled under my skin like worms:

"He made us eat our hearts." "She let us rot in the well." "They watched us bleed... for fun." "You're one of them, aren't you?"

I backed up into the corner, breath caught in my throat.

"No," I whispered. "I'm not. I'm not like them."

A soft cry echoed from the drain. A wet eye blinked up at me from inside it.

Suddenly, a hand shot out from under the tiles, **grabbing my ankle**, yanking me down.

The floor cracked.

I screamed as **a hundred clawed hands burst from the floor**, dragging me into the black beneath the bathroom tiles—sinking me into **a room that didn't exist**.

The Black Room Beneath

It was cold. Wet. Screaming.

Not aloud—but inside my head.

I was in a room made of bones. Tiny bones. Children's bones.

The spirits surrounded me—**not transparent**, but real, rotting, eyes missing, faces melted. Some were crawling on the ceiling. Some just stood, heads tilted, staring.

One of them came close.

A girl with half a skull. She reached for my face. Her fingers trembled.

"You're the last... You're the *key*..."

"What key?" I croaked. My voice cracked like ice.

"They made you... to open Hell."

And suddenly, all of them screamed at once.

"REMEMBER!"

The noise ruptured in my skull—**and I saw it.**

Fragmented Truth

Veer standing in a circle of fire, chanting in a language that bled shadows.

Elina, smiling while cutting her own skin and letting the blood drip into a baby's crib—**my crib**.

The Warden, burying dead students in the walls.

Mr. Yusuf... wasn't real. He was **a puppet**, made of ash and breath.

The third bed, glowing, **breathing**, with a shadow of myself lying in it —my evil self, already awake, already watching me.

I screamed. I thrashed. But the spirits **didn't hurt me**.
They held me still.
And one whispered, in the voice of a mother:

"You are not your father's child alone. You are still *hers*. Use what's left. Burn the curse."

I gasped for breath—and then I was back.

Back in the Bathroom
The tiles were whole. The mirror was fine.
But I wasn't.
My hands were bleeding.
A word had been scratched into my thigh with unseen fingers.
"REBELLION."

“I’m ready,” I told them, eyes glowing “ i am ready lets begin the ritual”

EPILOGUE

Epilogue

The Whisper Beneath the Bed

They thought I would disappear.

That once I was swallowed by the darkness, I'd be erased like the others —just another broken soul lost in the corridors of this cursed place.

But I'm still here.

I don't know how long it's been. Time works differently beneath the third bed. It coils and stretches like a serpent. Sometimes I hear voices—the girls, the boys, the ones I thought were real. Now I know the truth. They were never students. Just shadows. Puppets. Illusions crafted to corner me, to break me.

To awaken *her*.

The thing that walks beside me now wears my face. Her laughter is cold. Her eyes are black oceans. And she whispers all the things I once feared.

But I don't fear her anymore.

Because I understand her.

She's not my enemy. She's *me*—what they made me. What he made me.

Veer.

Elina.

The Warden.

They're watching. Always. Waiting for me to shatter. But I won't.

Because the dead… they've chosen me.

The spirits whisper secrets in my ears when I sleep. They curl around me in the dark. I used to think they wanted to hurt me. Maybe they still do. But they also want revenge.

They want justice.

And they want *freedom*.

This place, this hostel—it's a prison built on blood and bargains. And now, it's cracking.

So let them chain me.

Let them think I'm theirs.

Let them believe I've given in.

Because something far worse is coming.

And when I rise from the dark…

…I won't rise alone

…Because something far worse is coming. And when I rise from the dark… …I won't rise alone.

SCENE ENDS.

Cut to black.

But somewhere deep in the hostel…

A mirror quietly **cracks**.

Veer—sitting alone in his room—jerks his head toward the sound. The light flickers.

And then…

From beneath **his bed**… a whisper seeps out, slow and spine-chilling:

"You made me, father. Now watch me unmake you."

Black. End.

Acknowlegment

Acknowledgment

First of all, I'd like to thank my sanity for holding on… barely. To the coffee that fueled my demons, and the late nights when sleep was too scared to show up—this book owes you everything.

To my characters… especially Arya. You were *never* easy. You screamed, cried, fought, and made me question if I was writing you—or if you were writing me.

To Veer, Elina, and the Warden: thanks for being so horrifying that I had to keep my lights on while writing.

A special shoutout to my imagination—for being unhinged in all the right ways.

To the readers: If you've made it this far, congratulations. You're either brave, slightly unwell (like me), or both. Either way, I love you for it.

And to my future self… if you're reading this after the sequel, I hope you finally got that full night of sleep you kept dreaming about.